MY BIG FAT ZOMBIE FUN BOOK

MO O'HARA
and Dillon James West

ILLUSTRATED BY MAREK JAGUCKI

FEIWEL AND FRIENDS
NEW YORK

A FEIWEL AND FRIENDS BOOK

An imprint of Macmillan Publishing Group, LLC
175 Fifth Avenue, New York, NY 10010

Our books may be purchased in bulk for promotional, educational, or business
use. Please contact your local bookseller or the Macmillan Corporate and
Premium Sales Department at (800) 221-7945 ext. 5442 or by e-mail at
MacmillanSpecialMarkets@macmillan.com.

ISBN 978-1-250-12250-6 (hardcover)

Book design by Carol Ly

Feiwel and Friends logo designed by Filomena Tuosto

First edition, 2018

1 3 5 7 9 10 8 6 4 3 2

mackids.com

 TOM: Hi! Welcome to the pet fair! I'm Tom, and this is my best friend, Pradeep. We volunteered to be guides for the day, mostly because pets are awesome, but also so we can get away from our evil big brothers.

PRADEEP: Hey, what's your name?

YOUR NAME

TOM: This is Frankie. Once my big brother, **MARK**, tried to **TOXIC GUNGE** him, but we used a **BATTERY** to **SHOCK** him back to **LIFE**. Now he's a **FINTASTIC ZOMBIE GOLDFISH** with **HYPNO POWERS** and **GLOWING GREEN EYES**.

PRADEEP: See if you can find each of the bold words hidden in the letters below.

```
G Z G U G J C E M X P D P Q H
C O M R A J I J G V C O O S W
O M O P V U T S N N W X I E G
O B I L W J S Y S E U F U Q L
N I T Y X E A A R W D G N Q Y
G E E P L M T S I L G R E E N
P L Z Y I S N L O H K D X E A
G W O F F I G S O F A Y Z V
J B W W E R F P D I M E W K M
E N P W I N F K U O S W C L C
Y X B K E N C U N V Z O X W R
H T S C F O G P M H I K L N F
C I X O T A Y X B A T T E R Y
N G F H R H H C K Y R E N B Q
N K X S U I M M C M W K U Y B
```

TOM: No, Frankie! You don't have to hypnotize them! Now you're just showing off.

 PRADEEP: Can you understand what we're saying? Try to look between *swishy little fishy*.

```
SWISHYLIYTTLEFISHYSWISHYLITTLOEFISH
YSWISHYLIUTTLEFISHYHSWISHYLAITT
LEFISHYSWISHYLITTLEFISHYSWVISHYLIT
TLEFEISHYSWISHYLITTLEFISHYSWISHYLITT
LEFIBSHYSWISEHYLITTLEFISHYSWISHYLITTL
EFISHYESWISHYLNITTLEFHISHYSWIYSHY
LITTLEFISHYSWISHYLITTLEFISHYSWISHYPLI
TTLENFISHOYSWISHYLITTLEFISHYSWISHY
LITTLEFISHYSWISTHYLITITLEFISZHYSWI
SEHYLITTLEFISHYSWISHYLDITTLEFISHY
```

— — — — — — — — — — — —

— — — — — — — — — — .

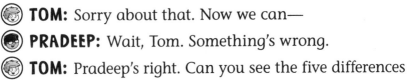 **TOM:** Sorry about that. Now we can—

PRADEEP: Wait, Tom. Something's wrong.

TOM: Pradeep's right. Can you see the five differences we're seeing?

MARK: Mwa-ha-ha-ha-ha-haaa!

TOM: I knew it! My big brother, Mark, is here with his pet vampire kitten, Fang. He's an evil scientist, if you couldn't tell from the laugh.

MARK: You morons better stay out of our way. We have *big* plans. You have no idea.

TOM: I think we have *some* ideas.

Mark partners with invading aliens to turn everyone into his mindless slaves.

Mark shoots Fang with a growth ray, and she tramples everyone in her path.

Fang tries to eat me . . . **again.**

Your idea:

5

MARK: Later, morons!

PRADEEP: Mark's right. We don't really know what they're up to, but it can't be good, whatever it is.

TOM: We definitely have to stop them. And if you're going to help, we have to make sure you're up to date on all our secret codes.

What color would we use for something like "Girls are nearby"?

A) Yellow   **C)** Orange

B) Blue   **D)** Red

What color would we use for something like "Somebody is murdering a goldfish"?

A) Yellow   **C)** Orange

B) Blue   **D)** Red

What's the walkie-talkie clicking pattern for "It's an emergency"?

A) • • — • • — • • • • —

B) — • — • • • — —

Which flag means "Someone's coming"?

A) World Cup Flag   **C)** Pirate Flag

B) Olympic Flag   **D)** Double Pirate Flag

Which flag means "Dangerous pirates"?

A) World Cup Flag   **C)** Pirate Flag

B) Olympic Flag   **D)** Double Pirate Flag

PRADEEP: Now for the most important part of *any* adventure preparation . . .

TOM: *Secret looks!* I'm going to give you some phrases. Draw the looks you'd make if you were saying them without actually saying them. Know what I mean?

I'm stuck in a booby trap, but I think I can cut my way loose with the sharp part of my keychain.

Frankie hypnotized the janitor, and he's pulling nasty green things out of the trash.

Mark is doing something evil, but we have to act normal or our parents will know something is wrong.

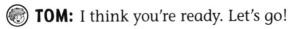

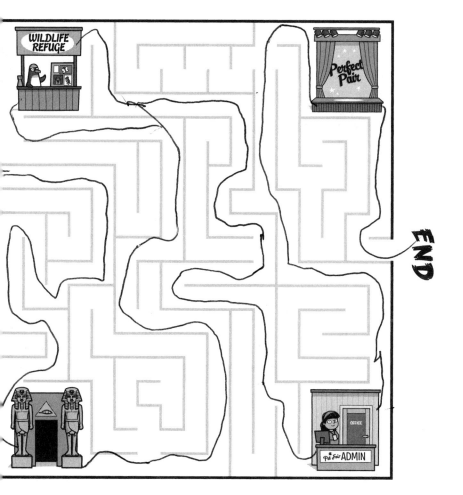

PRADEEP: The pet fair is *huge,* and we don't have time to backtrack. We should plan our route.

9

PRADEEP: Hey, Geeky Girl!

 GEEKY GIRL: Hey, guys. I'm starting an interest group for people with pets that have *special* abilities. I had a name for it, but for some reason, it's all scrambled in my head.

 PRADEEP: Hey, can you help by moving letters around to unscramble the words?

RALNPRAAOM STPE
STETRNIE GUORP

_ _ _ _ _ _ _ _ _   _ _ _ _

_ _ _ _ _ _ _ _   _ _ _ _ _

 GEEKY GIRL: Thanks. That was driving me crazy. I've been mixing up a lot of stuff lately. Want to try a few more?

EKEGY RILG   _ _ _ _ _   _ _ _ _

OIRBS EHT UGIDBE   _ _ _ _ _   _ _ _   _ _ _ _ _ _

CORNRE ROTES   _ _ _ _ _ _   _ _ _ _ _

CMTOUERP RCEAHK   _ _ _ _ _ _ _ _   _ _ _ _ _ _

CRIOAPNYCS   _ _ _ _ _ _ _ _ _ _

SAMI: Swishy little fishy!

 PRADEEP: Sami? What are you doing here?

GEEKY GIRL: She and Toby were the first pair to sign up for P.P.I.G.

PRADEEP: Where is Mom? Does she know you're missing one of your butterfly wings?

GEEKY GIRL: We can make you one, Sami. Boris, fly around and see if you can find some materials. Can you draw Sami another wing? Make it just like the first.

GEEKY GIRL: We made some fliers to pass around the fair. I bet there are tons of people who have awesome pets like ours.

 TOM: Um, you did actually *read* what you wrote, right? Or is this a new code I don't know about?

 GEEKY GIRL: It's not supposed to be a code.

PRADEEP: Can you figure out what they're saying?

P.P.I.G.

PARANORMAL PETS INTEREST GROUP

FOR PETS WITH SPECIAL, SUPERNATURAL, OR PARANORMAL INVESTIGATIVE POWERS.

_____ _____

_____ _____

___ ____ ____ _____'

_____ _____

_____ _____.

GEEKY GIRL & SAMI: *TECROMUP!*

PRADEEP: Now Geeky Girl *and* Sami are mixing things up. We have to find whatever's causing this.

TOM: See how many words you can make out of "TECROMUP." If we can figure out what they're saying, we might have a clue.

TECROMUP

_____   _____

_____   _____

_____   _____

_____   _____

_____   _____

PRADEEP: Something's wrong with Geeky Girl's computer. I think someone rewired it into a scrambler!

 TOM: But that would just scramble things on the computer, right? Why is it scrambling people too?

 PRADEEP: This is modified. If anyone's around it for too long, they start to get scrambled.

 TOM: What do we do? Do we have to destroy the laptop?

 GEEKY GIRL: *ON!*

 PRADEEP: We just have to rewire it. Draw new wires connecting A to A, B to B, and C to C. Make sure the wires don't touch each other, or you'll short the system.

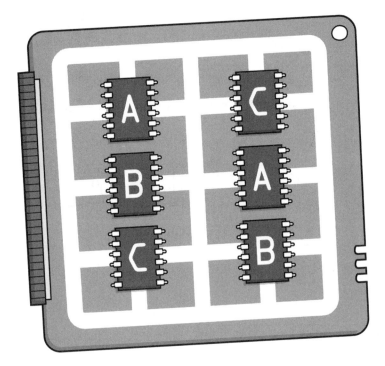

GEEKY GIRL: An IT guy borrowed my laptop earlier. I thought he was just checking the Wi-Fi, but he must have been making it into a scrambler!

TOM: Frankie thinks it's Mark. We know he's up to something, but this doesn't seem like his style.

PRADEEP: That's what I thought, but look. Color in the pixels set at zero.

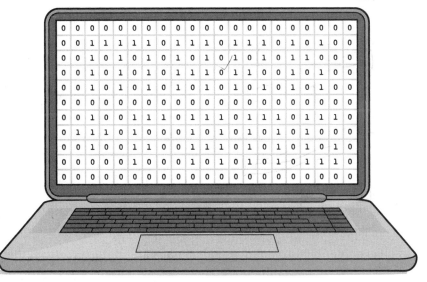

TOM: Come on. We have to find them before they scramble anyone else.

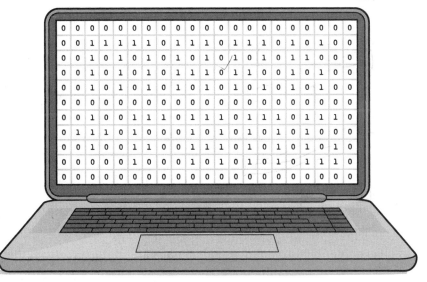

PRADEEP: Looks like Eel Bay and the Reservoir Water Sports Center teamed up.

TOM: They even built a replica of the lighthouse! Cool! Connect the dots from 1 to 43 and you'll see it.

LIGHTHOUSE KEEPER: Ahoy there, you little landlubbers. Welcome to the Lighthouse Games! The Electric Eel of Eel Bay is on display today!

TOM: Hey, Zarky!

 LIGHTHOUSE KEEPER: The eel is powering the scoreboard, but the blasted thing is on the fritz. See if you
young ones can turn off some of these lights by
coloring them in. Make the board say "HIGH SCORE."

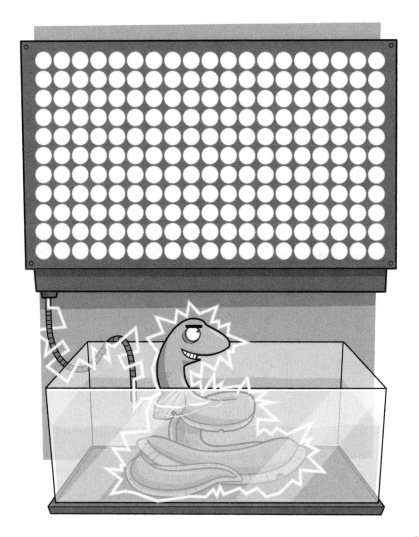

LIGHTHOUSE KEEPER: This game here's the Fish Toss. It's a tricky one. Grab one of these swordfish, close your eyes and jab your pencil at the scoreboard. After three tosses, add up your scores and see what you got. No cheating! I've got my good eye on you.

HIGH SCORE: _____

LIGHTHOUSE KEEPER: This one here's Paint the Tank. We'll cover your fish, there, in water paints, and they have to paint as much of the bottom as possible. Give it a go.

TOM: Without lifting your pencil, can you draw a path for Frankie to follow? He needs some help. Make sure it covers as many squares as possible without going through the same square twice.

LIGHTHOUSE KEEPER: When you're done, count up your squares, and you can see if you got them all.

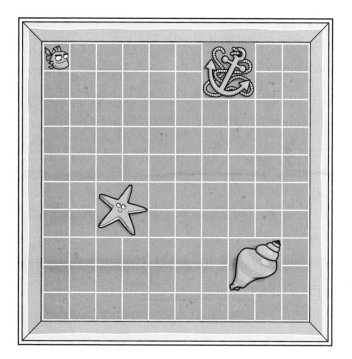

SCORE: ___ /88

LIGHTHOUSE KEEPER: This here's Water Golf. Set your ball in one of the starting places on the left, and then give it a good smack to the right.

PRADEEP: Your ball moves in a straight line unless

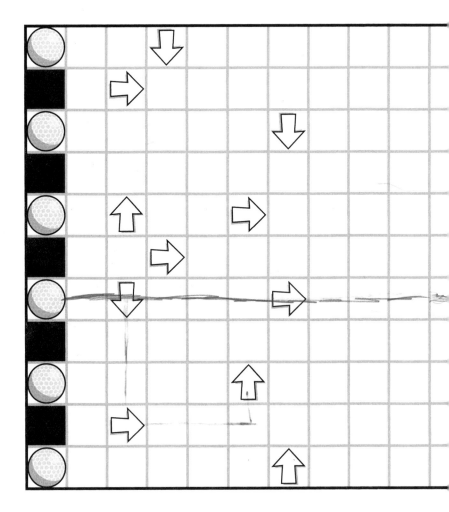

it hits something. When it does, follow the arrows and try to land in the goal.

 LIGHTHOUSE KEEPER: Mark how many tries it takes you. The fewer, the better.

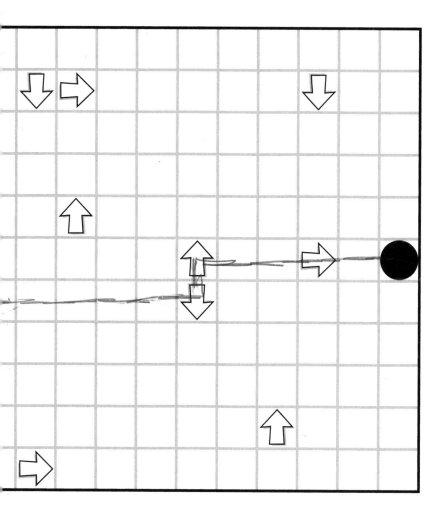

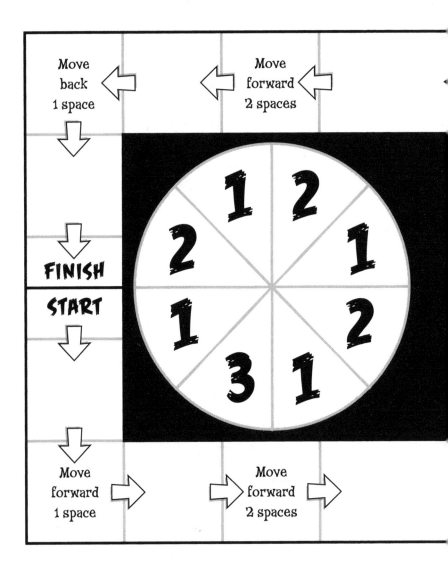

Move back 1 space

Move forward 2 spaces

FINISH

START

Move forward 1 space

Move forward 2 spaces

LIGHTHOUSE KEEPER: This here is our main event . . . the Jet Ski Race! Close your eyes and jab your pencil at the wheel to see how many spaces you move. Now you make sure you do what each space tells you to do. You've got to follow the instructions. Then start

Move forward 1 space

Move to Frankie

Move back 3 spaces

Move back 2 spaces

Move forward 3 spaces

Move back 1 space

Move to Frankie

Move back 3 spaces

your next turn. Reach the finish line as quickly as you can.

TOM: You can play with your friends too. Play Splash, Splosh, Grrr to see who goes first.

PRADEEP: Did we win? Put your scores on the board and we'll see.

SCOREBOARD

	FISH TOSS	PAINT THE TANK	WATER GOLF	JET SKI RACE
GROUP				
HIGH SCORE	1,000 points	150 points	-1	Finished yesterday

GEEKY GIRL: Something's wrong. There's no *way* anyone could get scores that high!

TOM: They must have lied about their scores!

SAMI: Pretty light is gone.

TOM: I bet it's Mark and Fang. We have to stop them! Can you color in the blocks to build a staircase from the bottom of the lighthouse to the top?

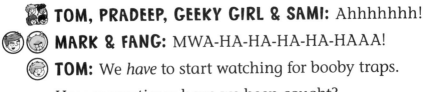

TOM, PRADEEP, GEEKY GIRL & SAMI: Ahhhhhhh!

MARK & FANG: MWA-HA-HA-HA-HA-HAAA!

TOM: We *have* to start watching for booby traps. How many times have we been caught?

PRADEEP: Draw a line through the rope from beginning to end. If we can figure out how it's knotted, I can undo the knot.

TOM: We're free!

MARK: Oh man! How did you morons do that? You were supposed to be tied up for the rest of the day!

GEEKY GIRL: Quick! Draw ropes and knots around Mark and Fang!

LIGHTHOUSE KEEPER: Thank you for catching these rapscallions. They might have gotten away with it too if it weren't for you not-so-pesky kids. Hee hee hee. Right, you can be off now. I know just what to do with these varmints.

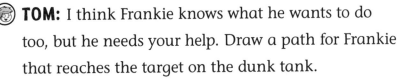 **FANG:** MEOW!

TOM: I think Frankie knows what he wants to do too, but he needs your help. Draw a path for Frankie that reaches the target on the dunk tank.

PRADEEP: Frankie can bounce and flip and do all kinds of tricks, so you can make it as tricky as you like!

 GEEKY GIRL: Now that Mark and Fang are taken care of, let's check out the Indie Booths!

GEEKY GIRL: These are the Indie Booths—short for independent. They crisscross all over the place, and they're filled with a bunch of people I think will be interested in P.P.I.G.

 PRADEEP: Fill in the boxes with the answers to our hints.

ACROSS

3. Molly the Invisible _____

4. Henry the Time-Traveling _____

6. Tap-Dancing Blue-Footed _____

7. Camille and her Tropical _____

DOWN

1. Charlie the Painting _____

2. Tugger the Magical _____

5. Siegfried and Roy the Roller-Skating _____

6. Fluffy the Psychic _____

30

SAMI: Henry!

 TOM: Is that the time-traveling hamster? It looks like he's trying to say something.

 GEEKY GIRL: Maybe he wants to join our interest group.

 PRADEEP: What do you think he's saying?

He's saying: _____

_____

_____

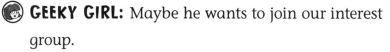

He's saying: _____

_____

_____

He's saying: _____

_____

_____

 TOM: Let's see if we can find his owner. Maybe they can translate.

31

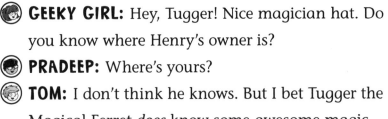

GEEKY GIRL: Hey, Tugger! Nice magician hat. Do you know where Henry's owner is?

PRADEEP: Where's yours?

TOM: I don't think he knows. But I bet Tugger the Magical Ferret *does* know some awesome magic tricks. Want to teach us one?

Grab a deck of normal playing cards. Make sure you have all fifty-two (but no jokers!). Divide the deck into four stacks, one for each suit: hearts, diamonds, clubs, and spades. Put each stack in order from the smallest number to the largest. Some of the cards have weird names, so if you don't know, the order is: Ace, 2, 3, 4, 5, 6, 7, 8, 9, 10, Jack, Queen, King. Put all the stacks on top of one another, and turn the whole deck facedown. Grab a bunch of cards from the top of the deck and set them to the side. Put the rest of the cards on top. This is called "cutting the deck." Cut the deck however many times you want. Make up a magic number. Use your birthday. Have your friend do it. Have all of them do it! When you're ready, deal the cards one at a time into thirteen stacks. Make sure you deal the cards in the same order every time. When you're done, you should have four cards in each stack. Now, flip them over! Every stack should have four cards with the same number. No matter how many times you cut the deck, the cards end up in the same stacks!

PRADEEP: Siegfried and Roy! Looks like they're working on some new roller-skating routines.

 GEEKY GIRL: By themselves. Where has everyone gone?

TOM: Frankie's zombie sense is kicking in. He thinks there's something up with the owners of the pets. It looks like the rabbits aren't doing so well on their own. Maybe we could help design some new routines for them.

 PRADEEP: Start on the edge and draw a fancy routine. When you're done, bring it back to the edge.

TOM: Hey, that's the blue-footed booby that dropped a booby trap on us!

PRADEEP: She also helped us beat Sanj, and she has an *excellent* tap-dancing routine. I think those make up for it.

GEEKY GIRL: Sounds more like Morse code to me.

PRADEEP: Wait. Maybe it *is* Morse code. Can you help us translate what she's saying? Here are my notes.

```
A ·—          I ··           P ·——·         V ···—
B —···        J ·———         Q ——·—         W ·——
C —·—·        K —·—          R ·—·          X —··—
D —··         L ·—··         S ···          Y —·——
E ·           M ——           T —            Z ——··
F ··—·        N —·           U ··—
G ——·         O ———
H ····
```

```
——  —·—·  —  ·—  ·——·

—··  ·—  —·  —·—·  ··  —·  —·—·  —··  ·  —  ·—  —·—·  ····  ·  ·—·

··  ···    ——  ··  ···  ···  ··  —·  —·—·


——  ———— ̄

——  —— —— ——  ——

——  —————·
```

GEEKY GIRL: So the tap-dancing teacher is missing too.

TOM: Maybe they're all just out to lunch or something.

SAMI: Bunny!

TOM: Good idea, Sami! Fluffy the Psychic Bunny might know.

PRADEEP: I don't think he can communicate as well as Frankie. Still, I guess it can't hurt to see what he can do.

Pick a number between 10 and 99. Add the two digits together and subtract that from your original number to get your **PSYCHIC NUMBER**. For example: 23. 2+3=5. 23-5 = Your Psychic Number. Find the symbol that matches your psychic number, then see which card Fluffy reveals!

⌘	→	⊙	◆	∼∼∼	✿	⁎⁎	✕	◈	✱	◑	☾	↕	◆	◈
0	1	2	3	4	5	6	7	8	9	10	11	12	13	14
∼∼∼	✕	◑	✱	↕	→	☾	◆	⊙	⌘	∼∼∼	✿	✱	⊙	⁎⁎
15	16	17	18	19	20	21	22	23	24	25	26	27	28	29
↕	◈	✿	☾	✕	⌘	✱	∼∼∼	⁎⁎	◑	→	↕	⊙	✿	☾
30	31	32	33	34	35	36	37	38	39	40	41	42	43	44
✱	∼∼∼	⌘	⁎⁎	✿	↕	◆	⊙	→	✱	◈	✕	☾	◑	⌘
45	46	47	48	49	50	51	52	53	54	55	56	57	58	59
◆	☾	⊙	✱	◑	◈	✕	∼∼∼	⊙	◆	↕	✿	✱	✕	∼∼∼
60	61	62	63	64	65	66	67	68	69	70	71	72	73	74
☾	⌘	⁎⁎	◆	✕	⊙	✱	◈	↕	⁎⁎	→	☾	✕	◑	✿
75	76	77	78	79	80	81	82	83	84	85	86	87	88	89
✱	✕	◈	↕	◑	→	∼∼∼	⁎⁎	⌘	✱					
90	91	92	93	94	95	96	97	98	99					

 TOM: Wow. He actually got it!

PRADEEP: That's amazing, but it doesn't tell us where the pet owners are. Even if they're just on break, we should keep looking to make sure.

GEEKY GIRL: Boris, why don't you do some reconnaissance? See if you can find Mark, Fang or the pet owners.

SAMI: Boris, take fliers too!

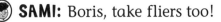

GEEKY GIRL: And pass out some fliers while you're at it.

TOM: Looks like Molly and Charlie have become friends.

PRADEEP: Molly can be a little hard to see. Connect the dots from 1 to 71 and you should be able to see her.

SAMI: Charlie paints.

PRADEEP: He specializes in French Impressionist sunsets.

TOM: Maybe he could teach us. How hard can it be?

KEY: 1: purple   2: blue   3: red   4: orange

TOM: You did a lot better than me. If you want, you can draw over mine. Turn it into something awesome, like with aliens or robots.

 PRADEEP: Sunsets aren't for everyone. What about comics?

 TOM: Definitely! We have all the supplies. Let's draw some comics!

41

TOM AND PRADEEP'S TOP TIPS FOR WRITING COMICS

1. Read lots of comics—if your parents complain, then just call it "research." They'll love that.

2. Go find things that you want to draw and look at them from different angles. Now, I'm not saying hang upside down from the Empire State Building or go roll over a hungry lion to get a better angle (although that would be very cool), but check out different pictures of things to give you ideas.

3. If you can't draw, then try again and again and again and again and ask for help, then try again. If after that you really can't draw, then find a friend who can.

4. Plan it out and "storyboard" your comic. (Pradeep is very good at this bit. I'm more of a draw-first-ask-questions-later kind of kid. But then there ends up being lots of questions.) To storyboard your comic just draw a bunch of boxes in a row, and then fill them in with what you want to happen in each box or panel of your comic. You can draw or write your storyboard.

5. Put in lots of action and show it in lots of different ways. Imagine you are directing a movie and you can have close-up shots, overhead view, long shots and split panels to show two things are going on at the same time.

6. Make it funny. (Pradeep says that comics don't have to be funny; they just have to tell a story, and that can be a sad story too. He even admitted to crying a little at the origin story of Captain Flopmonster.) But I still say mostly make it funny.

7. Think about what your characters say, why they say it and when. And make the characters' words—the dialogue—short.

Think about the beginning, middle and end for your story. Look at it like a mountain.

8. Only it's more interesting when you make your mountain harder to climb.

9. Read back your comic to see if it works. Even try reading it out loud, doing voices for the characters, like it's a play or something. That way you'll see if the characters all sound the same or if something doesn't make sense.

10. Show your comic to someone else, because you worked hard on it and now it's someone else's chance to read it and laugh (or cry). Good luck!!!

TOM: OK, your turn. Let's see what you can do.

GEEKY GIRL: I'm starting to think the pet owners have been kidnapped.

 PRADEEP: I don't think—

 TOM: Which means if we rescue them, we're pretty much secret agents.

 PRADEEP: That's not—

 GEEKY GIRL: Which means we need disguises! Draw a disguise for each of us.

🔵 **PRADEEP:** I'm not sure how these disguises are supposed to help.

🔵 **TOM:** They might not by themselves. We'll need **GADGETS** and **TUXEDOS** and **BRIEFCASES** with **SECRET** plans and a few **KUNG-FU** lessons. We'll have to go everywhere **INCOGNITO** until stuff starts **BLOWING UP** and we start **RUNNING** and **THWARTING BAD GUYS**.

🔵 **GEEKY GIRL:** See if you can find each of the words in bold.

```
P U G N I W O L B S B V W F B
B L E J U V H K O S R D C H D
I A P R M V U D W E I D Q A M
G S D Z B N E J K C E C P K L
T N N G X F V P R F H E B Q
S D I F U Y E J Y E C U Z W U
T R U T R Y H L B T A K O N I
E N M J R H S A P G S I C N F
G F A S N A L P N O E H C M B
D M Q T Q Q W N D N S O F B T
A F R Q R T M H B U G J V S K
G J R W T A Y R T N Y C F U B
H C X R W W G C I A Q I T M E
L P R O O S G T R U N N I N G
N V U S D G O S K U D W Z J D
```

PRADEEP: I think we should just keep moving.

TOM: Hey, Camille, what are you doing here?

CAMILLE: Hey, guys! I'm running a booth for tropical-fish appreciation. I *had* a game where people could try to identify the different species, but someone painted all my fish the same color. Now even *I* can't really tell them apart. Can you make each one of them look different?

 **SAMI:** Kitty!

 **GEEKY GIRL:** Fang is attacking the tank! Quick,
draw something that can stop her!

START

Sigfried & Roy
THE SKATING RABBITS

THE TAP-DANCING
BLUE-FOOTED BOOBY

FLUFFY
The Psychic Bunny

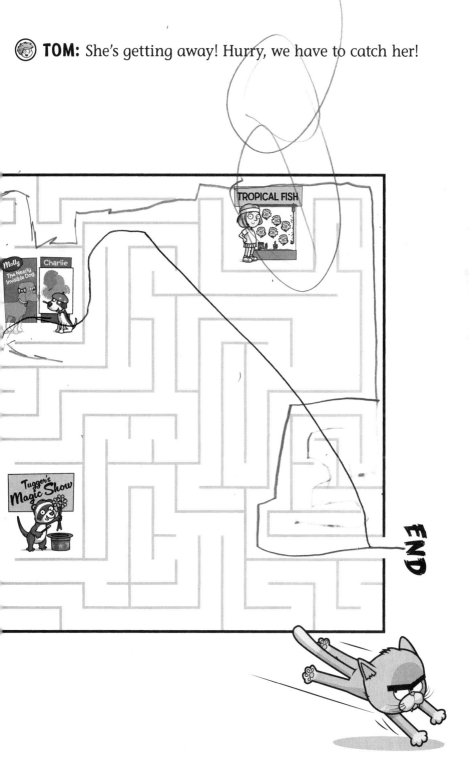

 **EVERYONE:** AAAH!

52

TOM: There are only a few things worse than getting soaked with water when you didn't expect it. Rank them from 5 to 1, 1 being the worst, and put *your* worst scenario at the bottom.

_____ Ending up suspended over a shark tank with hungry hammerhead sharks circling underneath you and the only thing that can save you is a telepathic octopus

_____ Trapped inside a sealed Egyptian tomb with a cursed stone and your mostly evil big brother and his totally evil vampire kitten

_____ Stuck up a tree with a hungry panther prowling below and only peanut butter pinecones to protect you

_____ Locked inside a medieval suit of armor with a zombie goldfish balanced on your head while riding a horse toward a big evil metal knight robot with a lance

_____ _____

_____

_____

(Your worse-than-being-doused-with-water scenario)

53

GEEKY GIRL: This is where Boris found the owners. Apparently they were all just shopping at the Pet Store Megabooth.

PRADEEP: Something doesn't feel right. Why did they *all* go shopping at the same time?

TOM: Plus, look at the signs! They're all mixed up. Help us unscramble these words.

PETSTORE

YUB TOW LSHEASE, TGE
NEO ERFE

___ ___ _____, ___
___ ____

PETSTORE

ERFE TEP SRTAET
THWI CEHPSAUR

____ ___ _____
____ _____

PETSTORE

EWN URMIAAQUS

___ _____

PETSTORE

WNE WEDRARS
RACD

___ _____
____

PETSTORE

EPT TEROS
OGBOMTHEA

___ _____
_____

GEEKY GIRL: There must be a scrambler nearby. Let's look around.

TOM: This booth is *really* big. Find a path that goes through every square without going through the same one twice.

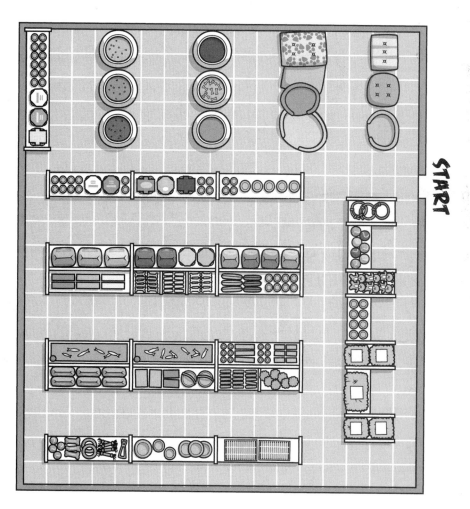

TOM: There are lots of people here.

PRADEEP: No one knows where they're supposed to be. Let's listen to them and see if we can figure out what order they should be in.

PRADEEP: Excuse me, ma'am? Do you need some help?

EMPLOYEE: Do you work here?

TOM: We don't, but you guys look like you could use some help, and we know a lot about pets.

EMPLOYEE: Oh, really? Prove it.

If you have a pet goldfish you need to keep him in fresh, clean . . .

A) water.

B) Jell-O.

C) toxic gunge.

If you are a pet sitter you need to . . .

A) actually sit on the pet the whole time you are watching it.

B) be responsible and look after the pet.

C) wander off and leave the pet alone.

Budgies can poop as often as every . . .

A) five hours.

B) hour.

C) twenty minutes (that's a lot of budgie poop!).

Kittens can sleep up to twenty hours a day.

A) True.

B) False.

C) True, but they are probably making evil plans in their dreams.

An octopus can squeeze itself into any space as long as its _____ fit(s) through.

A) beak

B) tentacles

C) large sombrero

EMPLOYEE: We do need help. If you're offering it, I'll take it. We've got a bunch of merchandise put back where it doesn't belong, and we need to get everything sorted.

 GEEKY GIRL: OK, Boris and I will handle the bird aisle. Tom and Frankie can take the fish aisle. Pradeep and Sami can go for the reptiles, and you can take the dogs. Just circle the items in each row that don't belong.

EMPLOYEE: My coworker borrowed the lockbox key from me, then ran off to lunch. I know they left it around here somewhere. Can you take a look?

EMPLOYEE: Argh! Everyone keeps talking about some stupid mega-sale, but we have no idea where they're getting that idea.

 GEEKY GIRL: It's all over your website. Look.

 EMPLOYEE: We didn't put that there! Can you cross out everything that has "sale" on it?

PRADEEP: If you didn't approve the sale, someone must have. Has anyone other than you used your computer?

EMPLOYEE: An IT guy came by to check the Wi-Fi.

GEEKY GIRL: I bet it's the same person who rewired my computer into a scrambler. They must have hacked into the website and added all the sales. But why?

PRADEEP: We'll need to rewire the computer. Just like last time: A to A, B to B, C to C and D to D.

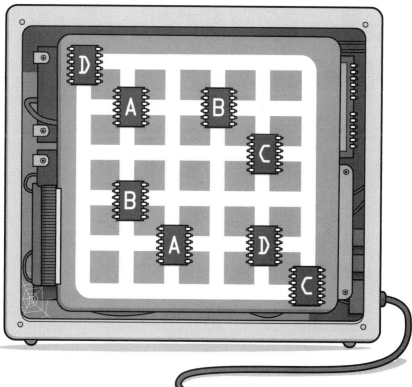

GEEKY GIRL: If you log in, I can see who modified your computer.

 EMPLOYEE: My boss is the only one with the password, and they're out to lunch. You can try guessing if you want.

PRADEEP: Make words by connecting the letters together, left and right, up and down or diagonally.

_____   _____

_____   _____

_____   _____

GEEKY GIRL: I think I've tracked down the name, but it's still behind some kind of code. Each number stands for one of two letters. See if you can figure out the right message.

1	2	3	4
A or N	B or O	C or P	D or Q

5	6	7	8	9
E or R	F or S	G or T	H or U	I or V

10	11	12	13
J or W	K or X	L or Y	M or Z

3 2 8 5 7 5 6 12   2 6

13 1 5 11   1 1 4   6 1 1 7

__ __ __ __ __ __ __ __   __ __

__ __ __ __   __ __ __   __ __ __

PRADEEP: I don't understand what Mark and Fang are doing. This doesn't feel like a *plan,* and Mark is all about *plans.*

 GEEKY GIRL: Maybe we'll find something in here. I saw it behind the computer.

 TOM: *Evil Scientist* magazine! That's got to have some kind of clue inside.

MAGAZINE: It's important to have the right tools for each evil plan. Match the evil plan on the left to the correct tool on the right.

1 Get inside a high-security bank vault

LARGE MECHANICAL CLAW

2 Make everyone get out of the swimming pool

SUCTION CUPS

3 Get to the top of a tall glass skyscraper

LAPTOP

4 Gain access to a news organization's private server

CHEMISTRY SET

5 Hold stupid little siblings away from your plans

LASER GUN

MAGAZINE: Your evil scientist brain is your *best* tool. What better way to sharpen it than devising some evil riddles to stump your stupid siblings? The best riddles are two to four lines long and end with words that rhyme. Give it a try!

EXAMPLE

Only one color, but not one size.
Stuck at the bottom, yet I easily fly.
Here in the sun, but not in the rain.
I do no harm and I feel no pain.

What am I?

RIDDLE #1

_____
_____
_____
_____

RIDDLE #2

_____
_____
_____
_____

RIDDLE #3

_____
_____
_____
_____

MAGAZINE: A good vocabulary is like a good evil laugh; no evil scientist is *really* evil without it. This month, we've invented five new evil words, and we want our readers to decide what they mean.

Trap-o-lishious

It means: _____

_____

Crima-pet-obot

It means: _____

_____

Splat-a-fish-inator

It means: _____

_____

Jazz-Evil-Science-ercise

It means: _____

_____

Evil-ali-doe-cious

It means: _____

_____

MAGAZINE: As cool as a really great evil laugh can be, you have to stay aware of your surroundings. Little morons could be thwarting your plans, and if you can listen *while* laughing, you'll be prepared. See if you can hear what they're saying inside the laugh.

```
MWAHAHAHAHAAAMWBAHAHAHAH
AAAIMWAHAHAHAHAAAMWAHAHA
GHAHAAAMWAHAHBAHAHAAAMWAR
HAHAHAHAAOAMWAHAHAHAHAAA
MWAHTAHAHAHAAAMHWAHAHAHEA
HAAAMWAHAHAHRAHAAAMWAHAHA
SHAHAAAMAWAHAHAHAHAAAMWRA
HAHAHAHAAAEMWAHAHAHAHAASA
MWAHAHAHATHAAAMWUAHAHAHA
HAPAAMWAHAHAHAHAAAMWAHIA
HAHAHAAAMWAHAHAHAHAADAMW
AHAHAHAHAAAMWAHAHAHAHAAA
```

— — —   — — — — — — — —

— — —   — — — — — — —.

MAGAZINE: It's important to familiarize yourself with your chemistry set, so you know when things go missing. Take a look at the two labs below. Can you see the five differences?

MAGAZINE: We're teaming up with the Evil Scientists-'R'-Us catalog to make a reader wish list. Describe your perfect evil gadget, and at the end of the month, we'll draw from a lottery and the winner will have their gadget made and sent to them.

Evil gadget name: _____

What does it do? _____

_____

What would you do with it? _____

_____

How much should it cost? _____

What does it look like?

MAGAZINE: With so much going on in our evil plans, it can be hard to keep everything straight. Here you'll find an evil plan submitted by one of our readers. See if you can put it back in the right order, starting with Step 1 and ending with Step 10.

BOB, DIABLO AND IGOR'S TEN-STEP PLAN
(WITH BONUS MAYHEM)
FOR CLOSING YOUR SCHOOL EARLY FOR SUMMER

_____ Take them to your evil scientist lab and place them into your "Croak-o-Matic 1000" Croak Extraction Machine (available in this issue of *Evil Scientist* magazine for only $19.99).

_____ Switch on the machine. (This was Igor's job.)

_____ Store all the extracted croaks in individual glass test tubes. Not plastic. You'll see why later. Mwa-ha-ha-ha-haaa.

_____ Find as many frogs and toads as you can. (Get your evil friends to help.)

_____ High-pitched note shatters the glass test tubes at the same time, releasing the croak gas into the air, which is inhaled by all the teachers.

_____ Make sure they are all near where the teachers normally stand.

_____ Take test tubes into school and place one in every classroom, including the library, gym and computer lab. Put a couple in the principal's office just to be safe.

70

_____ Teachers start croaking uncontrollably and can't teach.

_____ School needs to be closed because, literally, all the teachers have frogs in their throats.

_____ At a set time get someone to sing a super-high-pitched note over the loud speaker while singing the school song. (Diablo did this at our school. He has a scarily high range.)

_____ Release all the frogs and toads into the school cafeteria too. Just for fun.

Now your Evil Summer fun can start!! Mwa-ha-ha-haaa!

MAGAZINE: For our "Around the World" segment, we want to know: What are your Top 10 evil lair locations? Give each location a rank from 1 to 10.

_____ Volcano in the South Pacific

_____ Castle in the Northern Highlands

_____ Tower on the Windy Plains

_____ Laboratory Deep Underground

_____ Mansion in the Swiss Alps

_____ Military Base on an Undiscovered Island

_____ Death Ship in Deep Space

_____ Battleship in the Middle of the Ocean

_____ Skyscraper in a Big City

_____ Tree House in an Unexplored Jungle

MAGAZINE: It's time for the monthly Evil Scientist crossword! Place the words below into the boxes. Of course, we're evil, so no hints!

Words

Electricity	Kidnap
Laser	Lair
Scientist	Lab coat
Evil	Plan
Gunge	Chemistry

MAGAZINE: Outsmarting little morons gets easier when you get a lair, but a lot of evil scientists don't know what to do with a lair when they get one. This activity will help fuel your creativity. Choose a number between 1 and 10. Count down through the list until you reach your number. Cross out that item, and repeat until you have only five left.

Crocodile pit

Moving statues

Medieval armor

Supercomputer

Throne

Laboratory

Death ray

Spike traps

Security cameras

Servants

Shark-infested moat

Black cauldron

Skeletons

Zombies

Lightning rods

Coffins

Giant robots

Prison cells

Vault full of gold

Decorative banners

MAGAZINE: Now, draw your new Evil Lair!

 PRADEEP: There are a lot of activities about evil lairs.

TOM: Mark's always wanted one of those. I don't think that helps.

 GEEKY GIRL: We'll just have to keep looking.

TOM: I know just where to go. All this investigating stuff is making me hungry.

TOM: I can't believe they have a whole food court!

GLADYS: Well, hello there. Nice to see my favorite little goldfish again.

PRADEEP: Hi, Gladys. What are you doing here?

GLADYS: We **VOLUNTEERED** to help with the **BUFFET**. We've got all kinds of great food: **CHOC RICE POPS**, **WOBBLY EGGS**, **SALAD GREENS**, **BROCCOLI**, **TOAST**, **CARROT SOUP**. All the **BEST** stuff.

TOM: See if you can find each of the words in bold.

```
V S C D L B O E B M R X D D B
Y O N M Z O B N R B Q X A U X
I C L E F E H T O G X L F C Y
G D Q U E S W S C R A F T D Z
A J S R N E E C S E V O A A
K M F P Z T G B O T C Z R D I
W M O S G G E T L P O J R O U
P P Y G X Z X E I F U Q A H Q
S G A T L E C G R F B O C U O
D A B O B S S H O E I R S I A
K U F T H D L M O B D I E R D
Y L B B O W P M D C P C P J D
A M W M T O A S T S O E H H Z
O V H U I H U R S M Q D T L T
B G C J Q L F I D V L Q L O V
```

PRADEEP: I don't think we're interested. Thanks. I'm feeling a bit green.

 **TOM:** Hold on. We should get something for Frankie. Pick out the food Frankie would like. Do you remember what color food Frankie likes?

 GEEKY GIRL: Sami and I have to go get ready for the Great Pet Treat Bake-Off. We'll see you there.

TOM: Look, it's Antonio and Oddjobz!

 PRADEEP: I thought you guys were out on the ocean somewhere.

 ODDJOBZ: We couldn't miss the pet fair—or a chance to show off our cooking skills. If we can get this sign fixed, it's supposed to say "Sensational Sushi." Each number should be a different color.

KEY

0: White
1: Black
2: Gray

ODDJOBZ: Why don't you help Antonio with the sushi?

 TOM: I don't think Frankie is up for that.

PRADEEP: All that raw fish? Now I think Frankie is looking a bit green.

ODDJOBZ: How about you? The goal is to cut five pieces of sushi into at least sixteen small pieces using only three cuts. To make a cut, draw a straight line from any of the points around the edge of the board to any other point.

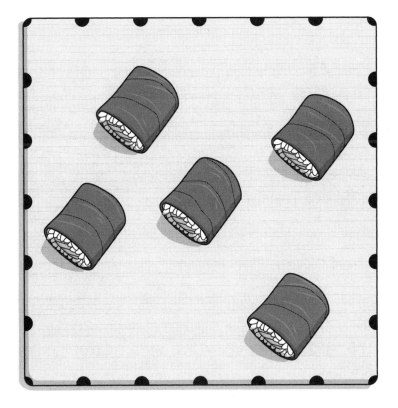

79

TOM: Can you make anything *other* than sushi?

ODDJOBZ: We hadn't planned on it, but I'm sure we could come up with something. I'll make up some names for the dishes, and you can tell us the ingredients.

007 Layer Salad   _____   _____

                   _____   _____

Umbrella-Bowl Soup   _____   _____

                   _____   _____

Incognito Nachos   _____   _____

                   _____   _____

Loco Meatloaf   _____   _____

                   _____   _____

Bowler Bread   _____   _____

                   _____   _____

Octo-Tofu Tower   _____   _____

                   _____   _____

Yacht Knots   _____   _____

                   _____   _____

ODDJOBZ: You should check out the Great Pet Treat Bake-Off. The finale is starting soon.

THE GREAT PET TREAT BAKE-OFF

 PRADEEP: We need a few things before the bake-off starts. Can you fill this out for us?

Zombie Libs

FOOD: _____

LIQUID: _____

COLOR: _____

SOMETHING SWEET: _____

NAME OF A DOG: _____

SIZE: _____

FOOD: _____

TYPE OF PET: _____

DESCRIPTION: _____

DESCRIPTION: _____

FOOD: _____

DESCRIPTION: _____

DESSERT: _____

WAY OF COOKING: _____

DESCRIPTION: _____

DESCRIPTION: _____

COLOR: _____

SOUNDS (MORE THAN ONE): _____

POWDERY FOOD: _____

GOOEY FOOD: _____

LIMB OF CAT: _____

INGREDIENT: _____

INGREDIENT: _____

PLACE IN A KITCHEN: _____

PLACE IN A KITCHEN: _____

PLACE: _____

TYPE OF CAKE: _____

SOMETHING YOU SHOUT: _____

SAME TYPE OF PET AS BEFORE: _____

COLOR: _____

GOOEY FOOD FROM BEFORE: _____

SOMETHING YOU SHOUT: _____

STORE: _____

TYPE OF CLOTHING: _____

DESCRIPTION: _____

WORD ENDING IN "EST": _____

THE GREAT PET TREAT BAKE-OFF

Smells of simmering _____(FOOD)_____ and bubbling _____(LIQUID)_____ filled the kitchen of the Great Pet Treat Bake-Off tent. Pradeep and Sami were in the finals along with Michael, who was making _____(COLOR)_____ _____(SOMETHING SWEET)_____ for his dog, _____(NAME OF A DOG)_____; Bella, who was making a very _____(SIZE)_____ _____(FOOD)_____ for her _____(TYPE OF PET)_____, and of course Mark and Fang.

Pradeep and Sami were attempting a very _____(DESCRIPTION)_____ dish. Toby was a very fussy eater. He only liked _____(DESCRIPTION)_____ _____(FOOD)_____ or _____(DESCRIPTION)_____ _____(DESSERT)_____, and only if it had been _____(WAY OF COOKING)_____.

They were going to make something that Sami was sure Toby would want to try though: a giant Ice Cream Lettuce.

Michael mixed up his ingredients and put them in the oven first. His dish smelled _____(DESCRIPTION)_____ and a little bit _____(DESCRIPTION)_____.

Bella tried to re-create her Giant Jell-O Jump and Eat. It won the _____(COLOR)_____ ribbon last year.

Mark and Fang seemed very secretive about their pet treats. They worked behind Mark's Evil Scientist coat, and we could hear lots of mixing and _____(SOUNDS)_____ coming from their table. They were covered in _____(POWDERY FOOD)_____ and _____(GOOEY FOOD)_____ by the end of the session, and Fang was licking chocolate off the tip of her _____(LIMB OF CAT)_____.

Pradeep and Sami worked very carefully. They mixed the _____(INGREDIENT)_____ and the _____(INGREDIENT)_____ together with the cream and ice to make their treat, but they couldn't find the lettuce they had brought with them. They looked in the _____(PLACE IN A KITCHEN)_____ and in the _____(PLACE IN A KITCHEN)_____ and even in the _____(PLACE)_____, but they couldn't find the lettuce.

It was time to present the foods and see how the pets liked their treats. Michael's ___(TYPE OF CAKE)___ came out of the oven and everyone said, "(SOMETHING YOU SHOUT)!" His dog seemed to love it.

Bella's ___(PET FROM BEFORE)___ got stuck inside her giant Jell-O after too much jumping and couldn't eat his way out. After he was rescued, he was last seen burping ___(COLOR)___ Jell-O all over the judges.

Mark and Fang were up next. They had made a beautiful pet-friendly chocolate and ___(GOOEY FOOD)___ mousse with kitten crunch crumble on top. Fang loved it.

Then the crowd suddenly shouted, "(SOMETHING YOU SHOUT)!" as Toby the tortoise walked out from behind Mark and Fang's table with an empty box of pet-friendly mousse with kitten crunch crumble topping balanced on his back.

The judges declared Mark and Fang's pet treat to be a fake.

"It's not ours!" Mark said, jumping up and down. "We definitely didn't buy that at ___(STORE)___ on the way here."

As he jumped, Sami and Pradeep's head of lettuce dropped out of his ___(TYPE OF CLOTHING)___ pocket.

"Meow!" said Fang as the two of them slunk offstage.

Pradeep and Sami quickly added the lettuce leaves to the ___(DESCRIPTION)___ ice cream. Even though Michael and his dog actually won the bake-off with their cake, as Toby ate the ice cream he looked like the ___(WORD ENDING IN "EST")___ tortoise ever.

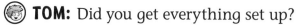 **TOM:** Did you get everything set up?

 **ODDJOBZ:** There's one thing left. You don't need a lot of heat when you're making sushi, so we didn't bring a stove. I can make one, but I could use some help with the wiring. Draw one line that hits all the points. Make sure you don't go through any space more than once. I don't want any explosions today.

ODDJOBZ: Something is wrong. Our customers keep saying something tastes rotten, but we're not sure what it is. Can you take a look?

There was something . . . jiggly . . . in my soup. I don't think it was supposed to be there.

What kind of restaurant serves rotten food?!

Was my meal supposed to be green? I didn't order a salad.

Whatever you put in this tasted terrible, and now I can't stop burping.

My husband's always had bad breath, but now it's unbearable. What was in this?!

TOM: Gladys, did you . . . um . . . give some of your wobbly eggs to Oddjobz?

GLADYS: I don't think so. Who is Oddjobz? Did he have something to do with our platters?

PRADEEP: What's wrong with your platters?

GLADYS: Someone mixed them up. Nobody but Linda knows how the things fit together, and she's taking her granddaughter to the bathroom.

TOM: Arrange the platters so they fit inside the buffet serving table without overlapping one another.

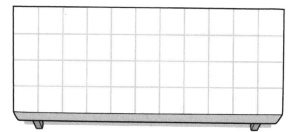

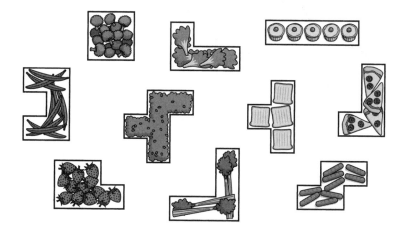

GLADYS: Now that you mention it, we *are* missing our eggs.

TOM: Frankie sees one!

PRADEEP: Me too!

TOM: I have an idea. Frankie, why don't you sniff them out . . . or whatever goldfish do that's like sniffing. Draw a path across the food court that goes through all the eggs.

MARK: MWA-HA-HA-HA-HAAA!

TOM: If Mark dumps the eggs into the soup, it will ruin the whole thing! Quick, draw something to stop him! Frankie can handle the rest.

MARK: Ow! Get this stupid fish off me!

GLADYS: Is this the young man causing problems? You are in big trouble.

ODDJOBZ: I'll say. This troublemaker nearly ruined Sensational Sushi . . . and other Culinary Cuisines.

GLADYS: And you are?

ODDJOBZ: Oddjobz. Pleased to me you. Now, I think we need to give Mark some work so he can start to make up for the chaos he caused, don't you? Put something nasty on these plates for him to wash. I want him to spend a *long* time on them.

TOM: Let's go. We should meet back up with Geeky Girl and Sami.

DR. McDOOM: Hello there, boys! Who's your friend?

 GEEKY GIRL: I'm the founder of the Paranormal Pets Interest Group.

 SAMI: P.P.I.G.!

 DR. McDOOM: Are you, now? I think I saw a flier for that. I'd join, but I don't think my pet will be making it to any of the meetings.

 TOM: If you didn't bring . . . your pet . . . what are you doing here?

 DR. McDOOM: I'm running a booth on ancient Egyptian pets! Maybe you can help me. I'm pretty sure this mural has something to do with a sacred Egyptian animal, but I don't know which one. Connect the dots from 1 to 53 and let's see.

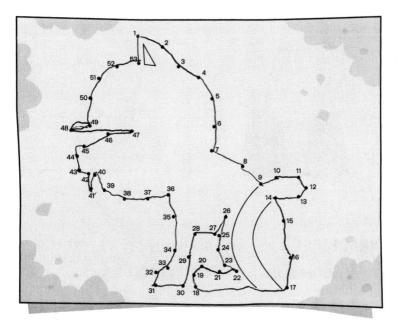

DR. McDOOM: I found these letters on some pottery from an old tomb. I had them translated from hieroglyphics, but the pots were shattered. I have no idea what order they were in. Make as many words as you can from TASBET, and maybe one of them will stick.

PRADEEP: We've seen this name before—when we were at the museum! It's another cat clue. . . .

DR. McDOOM: This is the sphinx, a mythical creature that was half-man, half-cat.

TOM: That sounds like Mark and Fang.

DR. McDOOM: I suppose it does. Legends say the sphinx would devour any traveler who couldn't answer its riddles. See if you can solve them.

I wake up.
I walk on four legs in the morning.
I walk on two legs at noon.
I walk on three legs in the evening.
I go to sleep.

What am I?
_____

Poor people have it.
Rich people need it.
If you eat it, you die.

What am I?
_____

Throw away my outside
  and cook my inside.
Then eat my outside
  and throw away my inside.

What am I?
_____

Take away my first letter,
  and I still sound the same.
Take away my last letter,
  and I still sound the same.
Take away my middle letter,
  and I still sound the same.
I am five letters long.

What am I?
_____

DR. McDOOM: This is a rock from Cairo. The excavators told me they think there's a fossil inside. Clean up the rock by shading in the areas the excavators have numbered. When you're done, we should be able to see inside.

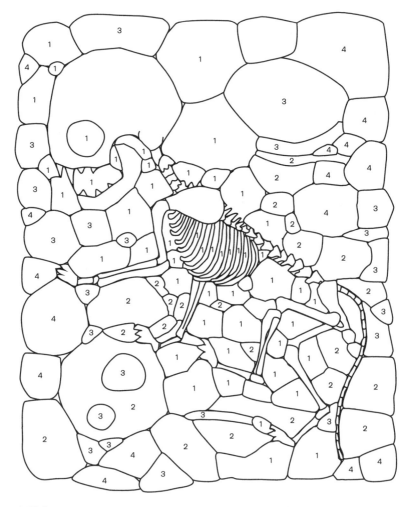

KEY: 1: Orange   2: Yellow   3: Red   4: Brown

DR. McDOOM: These are the pamphlets I've been handing out. They're filled with all kinds of great facts about Egyptian animal gods. Pretty cool, huh?

GEEKY GIRL: Um, Dr. McDoom? They're kind of . . . boring.

DR. McDOOM: They are? Well, maybe you can spice them up for me. Draw something to make my list of Egyptian facts more exciting.

Hatmehit was the goddess of life and looked a lot like a goldfish.

Ammit was called the "Kitten of the Dead" and looked like a crocodile, lion and hippo mixed.

Anubis was the god of the dead and had the head of a jackal.

Bastet was the goddess of cats and had

the head of a cat to prove it.

Horus was the god of the sky and might have looked like an angry budgie.

95

DR. McDOOM: This morning I received a very strange package. I don't know who it's from, but we should open it and find out. With just two straight cuts from edge to edge, slice through every strip of tape.

TOM: It was sent by "Secret Any Moose." What if it's some kind of secret evil moose organization that's trying to take over the pet fair?

PRADEEP: Or it could be that they spelled "anonymous" wrong? Just a thought.

TOM: OK, it could be that, but I'm still going to watch out for sneaky-looking moose too.

DR. McDOOM: These look like fragments of an Egyptian tablet. How exciting! I'll arrange the pieces like this, and you can draw what you think the missing pieces would have looked like.

PRADEEP: I'm starting to get a bad feeling about all this. Doesn't it seem a little . . .

TOM: Like something Mark would do? Yup.

DR. McDOOM: The package came with a letter, and it looks like Egyptian hieroglyphics! I don't suppose any of you can *read* hieroglyphics? I'm a bit rusty.

PRADEEP: Actually, we can. Let's take a look. The only tricky bit is that I don't remember which symbols are vowels.

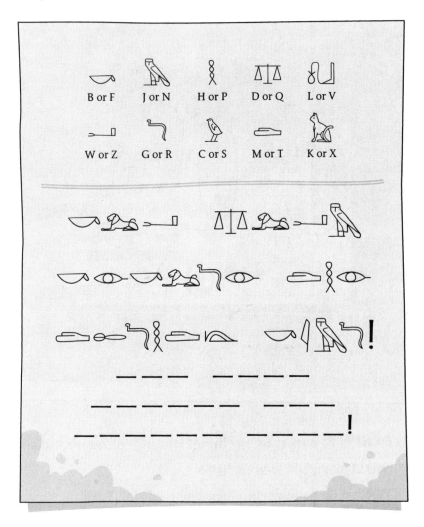

PRADEEP: LAL FO STIH PYGIAENT FTUFS SI KAFE! RAMK ASW HET NEO HOW TENS TI!

 **DR. McDOOM:** Is that some kind of ancient language?

TOM: Oh no! There must have been a scrambler in the package! See if you can figure out what Pradeep said while I find something to smash this.

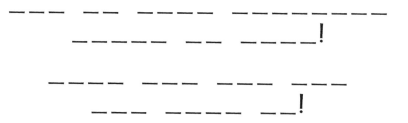

LAL FO STIH PYGIAENT
FTUFS SI KAFE!

RAMK ASW HET NEO
HOW TENS TI!

___ __ ____ _____

_____ __ ____!

____ ___ ___ ___

___ ____ __!

TOM: I smashed it on a rock. You should be OK now.

PRADEEP: We have got to stop Mark from spreading these scramblers!

 TOM: I don't think it's just him. I found these scraps of paper near the garbage can, but they look like Mark's handwriting. See if you can work out how they should join up, and we can tape the paper back together.

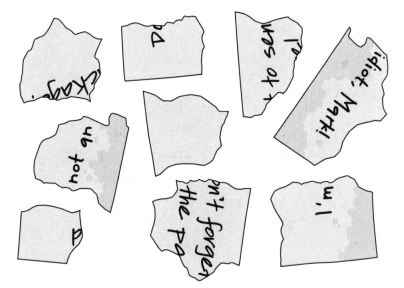

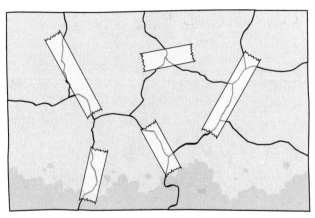

DR. McDOOM: So your big brother was behind all of this?

TOM: Looks that way. I'm sorry about your exhibit.

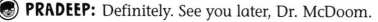 **DR. McDOOM:** I've got other projects to work on, especially the really *big* one you helped me with, remember?

PRADEEP: Definitely. See you later, Dr. McDoom.

TOM: I think Frankie wants you to say hi to your other "project" from him too. Bye.

DR. McDOOM: Hang on. This was an *educational* exhibit. It may not have gone the way I wanted it to, but I have to make sure you learned something.

The tomb of the Cat of Kings is guarded by:

A) the Jade-Necked Infiltrator
B) the Emerald-Eyed Protector
C) the Ruby-Bellied Eater
D) the Diamond-Haired Pursuer

How many hieroglyphics does it take to spell "cat"?

A) 3
B) 4
C) 5
D) 6

Egyptians kept servants in the tombs to:

A) protect them from ancient demons
B) argue with the God of Death
C) carry them back and forth between temples
D) take care of them in the afterlife

The Heart of Anubis . . . :

A) tastes awful
B) smells wonderful
C) looks boring
D) feels shocking

TOM: I wonder if he remembers us. Frankie hypnotized him pretty hard.

PRADEEP: We probably shouldn't bother him. He's

START

not evil anymore, and we don't want to mess that up.

 TOM: You're right. Let's check out this maze. Mark and Fang have messed everything else up. I'm sure he has some kind of evil plan for this.

GEEKY GIRL: Why don't we split up? I'll take Sami, and when you all get in trouble, we'll come rescue you.

SAMI: Hehehee!

(icon) **GRIZZLY:** Hey there, guppies!

(icon) **PRADEEP:** Grizzly Cook! What are you doing here?

(icon) **GRIZZLY:** I've been helping Sam Savage with his wildlife sanctuary, and I thought I'd use the pet fair as a good excuse to teach young campers the Rules for Survival in the Wild. See how many you can remember, and put your answers in the boxes.

ACROSS

1. You're not just lucky if you find some _____.
   If you're hungry, this plant can help hold you over.

2. Dart frogs are pretty; that's easy to see.
   But also they're poisonous, so tread _____.

5. Frostbite can occur when bare skin is _____.
   Take particular care of your fingers and toes.

7. Keep your group together and don't split up.
   You're safer in numbers if things turn _____.

8. If you cross a predator's path,
   don't make sudden movements or it might _____.

10. Singing and clapping when out on a hike
    means you won't surprise an animal and cause it to _____.

12. Always tell others where you're going and when you'll _____.
    That way if you're missed, searchers will know where to turn.

14. If you're by the ocean and need some food help,
    you can make a nice salad from seaweed and _____.

DOWN

1. Bring a jacket to wear should the weather turn _____.
   You'll be grateful for something to put on your shoulders.

3. Follow a stream when you're lost and _____.
Water can show you the way to head home.

4. When on a long hike, take time for breaks.
Exhausted people make awful _____.

6. Some mushrooms are yummy, but some contain _____.
If you can't tell the difference, it's best to avoid them.

9. If you are lost or scared or hurt, your whistle can raise the _____.

11. When things go wrong, you'll want to _____.
Instead stop, relax and try to think.

13. Morning food is your fuel and your survival _____.

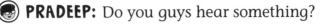 **PRADEEP:** Do you guys hear something?

TOM: I feel like we've heard that before.

GRIZZLY: You have. Can you figure out what it is?

Look for five differences between these two pictures.

TOM: It's the Beast of Burdock Woods! She's a *lot* bigger than when we last saw her.

GRIZZLY: She's definitely grown up. She's also definitely supposed to be wearing a leash and collar with bells on it.

PRADEEP: Why the bells?

GRIZZLY: Without them, we lose track of her. She's *really* sneaky, but Sam insists on bringing her everywhere. Can you figure out how to make her more noticeable?

GRIZZLY: All right, mates. Round two. This time, we'll keep things pet-themed. It is a pet fair, after all. Match the beginning of each rule with the right end.

In critters will creep	What does its bite do? Well, trust me. It's gross.
Never try to outrun a bear.	Leave it alone. Give it a rest.
Critters with cubs will always protect them,	if you store food where you sleep.
Never touch anything in a bird's nest.	He's faster than you, so don't you dare.
If you see a night animal during the day,	it could be sick with rabies, so keep far away!
Fire salamanders are full of venom.	but the males have venomous spikes in their feet.
Rattlesnakes rattle when you get too close.	so don't pick one up and don't try to pet 'em.
The platypus looks so cuddly and sweet,	Best stay far away and don't try to inspect them.

TOM: Are you sure these are about *pets*?

PRADEEP: Have you seen Mark in the wildlife maze?

TOM: Or a really cute but *totally* evil little kitten . . . with fangs?

GRIZZLY: You're talking about that troublemaker from the camping trip? I can't say that I have. Why?

TOM: He's been hatching evil plans, breaking things . . . you know, big-brother stuff.

GRIZZLY: And you think he's going to do something to the wildlife maze? What could he do in here?

HE COULD: _____

_____

_____

GRIZZLY: What happened here?!

PRADEEP: It looks like someone clawed through the maze.

TOM: And by "someone," we mean a really cute but *totally* evil little kitten . . . with claws.

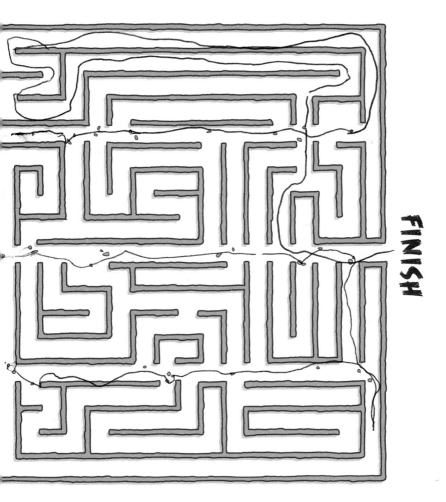

GRIZZLY: We have to fix the maze. Otherwise, people can just walk straight to the finish, and they won't learn anything about surviving in the wild. Fill in the gaps in the maze walls so that there is only one path to the end.

FINISH

TOM: I think we have a problem.

PRADEEP: Someone blocked the exit to the maze!

GEEKY GIRL: Hey, are you guys in there?

PRADEEP: Yeah. Is Sami still with you?

SAMI: Here!

GEEKY GIRL: We'll throw you some blocks over the wall. Color in twenty-three blocks to make something you can use to climb over the wall.

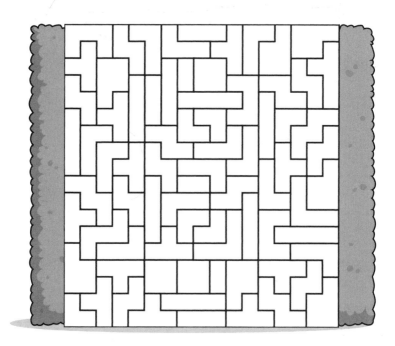

GEEKY GIRL: Once you're over, we should head for the administration building. Something suspicious is going on.

PRADEEP: This place is a mess! You'd think an administration building would be more . . . *orderly.*

GEEKY GIRL: Does anyone know what's going on here?

ADMINISTRATORS: GITNAYWUE!

SAMI: More scrambles.

TOM: Sami's right. We'll look for the scramblers. You try to figure out what they're saying.

PRADEEP: Make words or phrases by connecting the letters together: left and right, up and down or diagonally. You can't use the same letter more than once per word or phrase.

_____   _____

_____   _____

___ ___ ___ ___ ___ ___ ___ ___ ___

TOM: Don't worry, everybody. We're the *new* new IT guys. We'll get everything fixed so you can get back to work.

GEEKY GIRL: We have to find all eight computers and smart devices.

PRADEEP: We'll rewire the smaller computers. You take this big one. Connect A to A, B to B, C to C, D to D and E to E. Like before, make sure the wires don't touch one another.

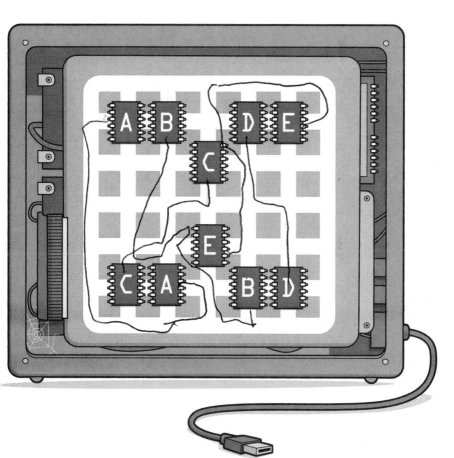

ADMINISTRATOR: Idd ouy xfi ti?

 TOM: Why are they still scrambled? I thought we fixed all the computers.

GEEKY GIRL: We must have missed one. We'll need to build a scrambler tracker to find the source. It must be a pretty powerful signal, which means we can detect it.

PRADEEP: Help Geeky Girl design a scrambler tracker. What do you think one of those would look like?

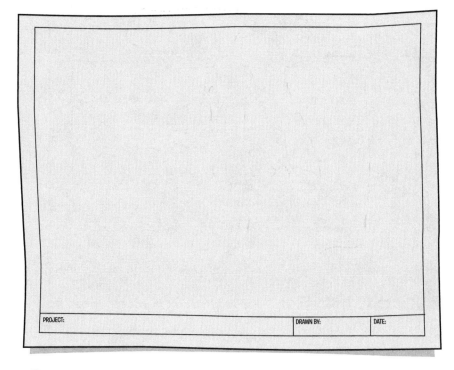

PROJECT: DRAWN BY: DATE:

GEEKY GIRL: I'll get to work on this. Once it's built, we'll just have to wait until we get some kind of signal.

WOOOSH, FLIP... CLUNK!

 PRADEEP: Sami, I think Toby has flipped over again from his levitating and can't roll back.

 SAMI: Poor Toby. Toby misses tele-popping.

 GEEKY GIRL: Yeah, I bet. He hasn't really got the hang of his new levitating power after the TV show power swap happened. I guess tortoises aren't naturally built for speed.

 PRADEEP: How is Boris getting on with his teleporting?

GEEKY GIRL: He still gets some . . . what did you call it, Sami?

SAMI: Tele-popping Tummy.

GEEKY GIRL: Yeah, tele-pop . . . I mean teleporting tummy when he pops around too much. And he really misses flying.

Wooosh, FLIP... CLUNK.

Squuuui ... POP.

 GEEKY GIRL: Boris, you popped back. Could you just nudge Toby again so he's right side up?

Clunk ... FLIP.

 GEEKY GIRL: Thanks, Boris.

TOM: Hey, everyone, I've picked up a reading. We've tracked the signal scrambler booster to this room in front of us, but we can't get inside.

 SANJ: Go away. There's absolutely no one in here.

PRADEEP: That's Sanj's voice! I knew it was him!

 GEEKY GIRL: Yo! Evil dude! We know it's you, and we know you're in there. Come out now and give yourself up.

SANJ: Or what?

 SAMI: Or I'll tell our mommy.

SANJ: Mom thinks I'm away at boarding school. She won't believe you, and besides, by the time you do that it won't matter because my plan will be complete. Mwa-haa-heee-hee-ahhh-haa-weeeeeeeze.

TOM: He never did get that evil laugh down, did he?

GEEKY GIRL: Open up!

SANJ: I can see you on the security cam. Upper left-hand corner. Give a little wave. You just have four little moron kids and a couple of pathetic pets. Oooh, I'm so afraid. What can you do?

 **SAMI:** We can. We can stop you, Sanj.

SANJ: Now please stop disturbing me; I've nearly finished aligning everything to stabilize the power export for the booster. I'm a very busy Evil Computer Genius, you know. Go away.

TOM: Sanj is right. We can't break down the door, and by the time we go get help, his evil plan will be complete. If only we could get in some other way. . . .

PRADEEP: The building plans for the convention center! There might be another way into the room. Geeky Girl, can you bring them up on your computer?

GEEKY GIRL: I'm on it. . . . Got it! Yes! There's an air vent that goes through the ceiling around this floor. We could get in that way.

TOM: Yes, we can get Sanj!

PRADEEP: Um, is that map drawn to scale?

GEEKY GIRL: Yes.

PRADEEP: Then we need to be about Action Man–size to crawl through there. It's no good.

SAMI: Or Action Tortoise–size.

TOM: You mean, send in Toby? But he isn't that stable with this power. What if he just gets stuck upside down in the air vent?

GEEKY GIRL: Then Action Budgie will go with him. They can do it together.

GEEKY GIRL: Draw a line through the blueprints from Boris and Toby to Sanj.

TOM: Thanks. You got them to the right room. Phew. Now can you hear anything? Are they inside yet?

PRADEEP: All I can hear is Sanj breathing heavy. He does that when he's really concentrating. I bet he's sticking his tongue out the side of his mouth. He does that too.

GEEKY GIRL: Hang on, what's that noise?

WOOOOOOOSHHHH!

KEEEERRRPLLLUUUUNK!

HOLY BOOMERANGING BUDGIES!!!

ZIIIIIIIP, FIZZZZZZ,

POING!!!!!

KABOOM!!!!!!!!!!!!

PRADEEP: I hear footsteps.

CLICK, CLACK, CLUNK.

 SANJ: A budgie?? And a tortoise??? It's so humiliating.

 GEEKY GIRL: Boris! You have your levitating power back!

Squiiii-*POP!*

 SAMI: Toby is tele-popping again! Yaaay!

 SANJ: They smashed into the scramble disruption dish just as it was powering up. It caused the explosion.

 PRADEEP: That could have caused a reversal in the previous parameters that transferred their particular powers.

 TOM: And in English?

 PRADEEP: It swapped the powers back to normal.

 TOM: Good work, everyone. Now let's get Sanj out of here. Come on. We still have to track down Mark and Fang!

TOM: I'm glad Sanj is out of the way, but we still don't know what he was doing with all those scramblers.

 GEEKY GIRL: We should check his computer. Maybe he kept a log.

 PRADEEP: He's an Evil Computer Genius, so it's going to have a *lot* of security measures. To start, we have to figure out what letters he's using for his password. Can you see them?

BIGBROTHERRSEVILDEEDSTOLITTLE
ANNOYINGMORONSBBIGBROTHER
SEVILDEEDSTOLITTLEANNOYINGM
MORONSBBIGBROTHERSEVILDEEDS
TOLITTLEANNOYINGMORONSBIGB
ROTHERSEVILLDEEDSTOLLITTLEANN
OYINGMORONSSBIGBROTHERSEVIL
DEEDDSTOLITTLEEANNOYINGMORONS
BIGBROTHERSEEVILDEEDSTOLITTLEA
NNOUYINGMORONSBIGBROTHERSEVI
LDEEDSTOLITTLEAANNOYINGMORONS

GEEKY GIRL: OK, now make as many words or phrases as you can out of those letters. We're looking for something Sanj would use as a password.

_____

_____

_____

_____

_____

_____

_____

_____

_____

_____

PASSWORD: _ . _ . _ . _ . _ . _ . _ . _ _ _ _

GEEKY GIRL: We're in! I found the logs for Sanj and Mark's evil plans, but even these are scrambled. I think I can get most of the letters back in the right order, but you'll have to put the plan in order from 1 to 10.

THE PERFECT EVIL PLAN FOR RUINING THE PET FAIR

STEP # [ ] Turn the administration computers into a giant scrambler. This is really just a pet project (HA!), but if I can put together a giant scrambler, then NOBODY will be able to think straight, and we can get away with whatever we want! Plus it will make the final contests even easier for Mark and Fang.

STEP # [ ] We sell the golden trophy for cash, and add that to the prize money. Then we add that to the money we've saved up from all our other stuff and the money Mom and Dad think is going to boarding school.

STEP # [ ] Gain access to everyone's computers, especially that one girl. I think Dad has an old IT-repair-guy badge somewhere that can help with that. No one ever really looks at the IT guy, and they give them access to everything. Morons!

STEP # [ ] Mark and Fang cause chaos in the pet fair: hatching evil plans, breaking things . . . you know, evil scientist stuff. Nobody will think to look for me with everything else going on, especially when I sign everything with "Mark and Fang."

STEP # We get in touch with *Evil Scientist* magazine and buy the best evil lair they can design. Crocodile pit, supercomputers, death rays, everything. We won't have to work out of my parents' garage anymore, which is great because it's kind of starting to smell in there.

STEP # Do something nasty to the computers. I'm thinking some kind of scrambler, but I don't want to scramble just the electronics. Everyone's so busy with their pets, they probably wouldn't use their computers much anyway. BUT if I modify the signal and rewire a few of the components, I think I could scramble their BRAINS!

STEP # Get inside the administration building. The IT badge should be enough to get me through, but just in case, I'll send a little virus ahead of me. Something nasty enough for them to call the repair guy, and BAM, I'm in.

STEP # Hack into the pet store's computer. We need to keep the adults busy, so I'll set up some kind of mega-sale. I'll send a notification to everyone's phones, and when they run away to buy things, it gives Mark and Fang time to cause some trouble.

STEP # The pet fair ends with the Perfect Pair Contest. The best pair at the fair gets a golden trophy and a cash prize. Mark and Fang use all the stuff we've done to prove they're the perfect evil pair, and they're sure to win. No one, even our moron little brothers, can stop the judges from voting for Mark and Fang, especially with Mark's recent . . . acquisition.

STEP # Get past those morons at the entrance without them seeing me. I'll wear some kind of disguise . . . maybe something with a mustache. Everyone thinks I'm at boarding school, anyway, so it's not like they'll be looking for me. I'll tell Mark to make a distraction just in case.

STEP # Take over the world.

TOM: So all we have to do is **STOP MARK** and **FANG** from **WINNING** the **BEAUTY CONTEST**, the **ATHLETIC COMPETITION** and the **PERFECT PAIR JUDGING**. If we don't, they'll **TAKE OVER** the **WORLD**.

PRADEEP: They've been one step ahead of us all day. I don't know if we can stop them in time.

TOM: Well, at least Frankie looks confident.

```
W F H T H X N W Y C X N F J K
G I A S F H P U R T Z I U R F
C K N F J E I L L I U U Z I L
E O Z N R Y B P J F Y A Z F Z
E W A F I G H Y X F N C E S U
Z K E N U N Y X H O A O B B W
F C M A R K G H I D K N M E W
T D R E V O X T B N Y T G A Z
Y L D J P K I A T H L E T I C
E R J H O T M G M T S S I E X
S O I L E S V Q C I F T Y B B
Q W G P L F L G N I G D U J P
X F M S S C C H S H M L N O A
I O Y I F N S C V A N L T Z I
C I P H K L F V C V Z S U I R
```

128

PET BEAUTY CONTEST

 TOM: Let's get ready for the beauty contest. Here's what we need:

Zombie Lib

THINGS (MORE THAN ONE): _____

SIZE: _____

COLOR: _____

THING THAT SPARKLES: _____

ANIMAL: _____

ANIMAL: _____

DESCRIPTION: _____

THING: _____

ACTION: _____

WORD ENDING IN "LY": _____

EXOTIC OR RARE ANIMAL: _____

THING: _____

ACTION ENDING IN "ING": _____

TYPE OF MUSIC: _____

HAIRSTYLE: _____

TYPE OF CLOTHING: _____

DESCRIPTION: _____

THING THAT SPARKLES: _____

DESCRIPTION: _____

THING: _____

THING WITH WHEELS: _____

SAME EXOTIC ANIMAL AS BEFORE: _____

THING: _____

WORD ENDING IN "LY": _____

SOMETHING YOU SHOUT: _____

DESCRIPTION: _____

DESCRIPTION: _____

ACTION ENDING IN "ED": _____

DESCRIPTION: _____

DESCRIPTION: _____

THING THAT IS SOFT: _____

SOMETHING YOU SHOUT: _____

SOMETHING YOU SHOUT: _____

DESCRIPTION: _____

PET BEAUTY CONTEST

"Attention pets and your ___(THINGS, MORE THAN ONE)___," said the lady with ___(SIZE)___ ___(COLOR)___ hair. "The Annual Pet Beauty Contest is about to start. The winner will be awarded this Most Beautiful Pet sash and ___(THING THAT SPARKLES)___ crown."

"Could all pets please come to the catwalk?" she continued. "I know that some of the ___(ANIMAL)___ owners and ___(ANIMAL)___ owners complained about it being called a "catwalk," but it does not mean we are biased toward cats."

"Please bring your ___(DESCRIPTION)___ ___(THING)___ with you, and don't forget to ___(ACTION)___ ___(WORD ENDING IN "LY")___ as you step out on the stage."

Frankie and I lined up on the steps next to a ___(EXOTIC OR RARE ANIMAL)___, a dog wearing a ___(THING)___, a lizard that was ___(ACTION ENDING IN "ING")___ to ___(TYPE OF MUSIC)___ and a goat wearing false eyelashes and ___(HAIRSTYLE)___.

Frankie had already decided to wear a ___(TYPE OF CLOTHING)___ for the contest but said no to wearing Sami's ___(DESCRIPTION)___ tiara. I don't think he was taking this beauty contest seriously.

First up was Toby, Sami's tortoise. She had decorated him with ___(THING THAT SPARKLES)___ all over his shell and he wore a ___(DESCRIPTION)___ ___(THING)___ on his head. Toby had to be rolled down the catwalk though, on a ___(THING WITH WHEELS)___ because he was too shy to walk down himself.

"Awww." The crowd sighed.

It was the lizard's turn next, but suddenly Fang jumped over the ___(EXOTIC OR RARE ANIMAL)___. She swiped the ___(THING)___ off its head, swung off the winner's sash that the lady with the microphone held and landed (WORD ENDING IN "LY") on the catwalk.

"(SOMETHING YOU SHOUT)! That ____(DESCRIPTION)____ kitten is ruining the show!" shouted the lady with the microphone. She threw the winner's sash and ____(DESCRIPTION)____ crown at Fang and ran off the stage screaming.

As soon as the goat saw the sash and crown flying through the air she immediately (ACTION ENDING IN "ED") down the catwalk. Fang was so busy playing with the ____(DESCRIPTION)____ sash, she didn't see the goat coming, and it bumped her right off the stage and into the ____(DESCRIPTION)____ (THING THAT IS SOFT). Lucky it was a soft landing.

"(SOMETHING YOU SHOUT) for the goat! ____(SOMETHING YOU SHOUT)____!" shouted the crowd.

The goat then fluttered her eyelashes as she caught the Most Beautiful Pet winner's sash in her teeth, and the crown landed right between her two ____(DESCRIPTION)____ horns. She gobbled up the sash straightaway, but I think she liked wearing the crown.

TOM: Hey, Sebastian. Hey, Guinevere.

SEBASTIAN: Hello, everyone. We were about to start the Olym-Pets!

PRADEEP: Olym-Pets?

SEBASTIAN: It's short for . . . never mind. It's a pet athletics competition. Are you guys participating?

TOM: Yeah. We have to beat my big brother, Mark, before he wins and buys an evil lair and takes over the world.

SEBASTIAN: OK, then. Why don't you light the official torch. Draw a big official-looking fire on Guinevere's torch.

SEBASTIAN: Our first event is the obstacle course. Pick a starting spot on the left and move to the right. When you hit something, follow the arrows to change directions. If you pick the wrong starting spot, start over with a different one.

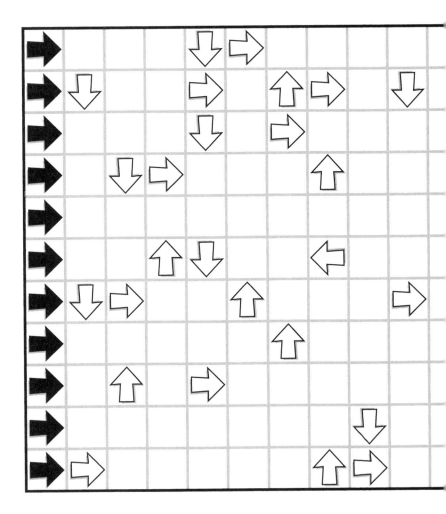

MARK: We've already finished. You'd have to finish in less than three tries to beat us, and little morons with stupid pets have no chance.

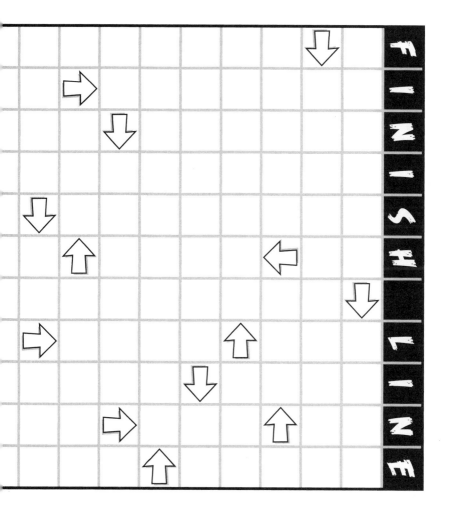

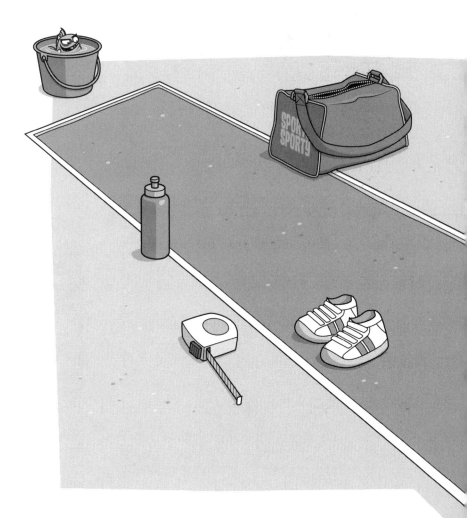

 SEBASTIAN: Our second event is the long jump. Take one jump to go as far as you can.

TOM: We have to get past Mark, but with Frankie, that should be easy. Draw a path from Frankie to somewhere past Mark. Use some fishy techniques if you have to: bounce, spin, whatever. Just make sure you don't touch the ground.

SEBASTIAN: Our final event is the four-hundred-meter dash! Take your places, everyone!

 MARK: Your stupid fish is going down. How could he possibly beat the fastest little evil kitteny-witteny in the world?

 FANG: Meow. . . .

TOM: Close your eyes and jab at the wheel to see how many spaces Frankie moves. When you're done moving, follow the instructions of the space you land on.

 MARK: Yeah, then all Fang has to do is move the same number of spaces plus one. We can't lose. Losers!

 PRADEEP: That's not true. It's hard, but you can win.

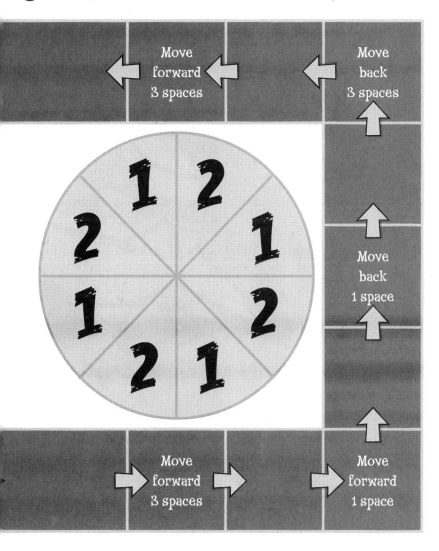

TOM: Did we win?

SEBASTIAN: We won't know until the end of the day. The scores are submitted as part of the Perfect Pair Competition.

PRADEEP: Mark probably faked his scores here too.

SEBASTIAN: Maybe, but I have a feeling that won't mean as much as he thinks. Chivalry is a big part of any good competition, and you remember what that means, right?

Chivalry is one of the _____.

A) Principles of Knighthood   **C)** Laws of Competition
B) Articles of Adulthood   **D)** Essays of Robin Hood

It means one should be _____.

A) smart and overly complicated   **C)** pompous and noble-born
B) gallant and well-mannered   **D)** friendly and intrusive

Refusing to toast your host with a cupful of goldfish is _____.

A) very chivalrous   **C)** more chivalrous than most people
B) kind of chivalrous   **D)** very unchivalrous

If you think someone is cheating, the chivalrous thing to do is _____.

A) absolutely nothing   **C)** report it to the judges
B) cheat more than they do   **D)** refuse to compete

A chivalrous person bows before a _____.

A) princess   **C)** queen
B) lady   **D)** A, B and C

TOM: Thanks, Sebastian. We have to go if we're going to make it to the judging.

SOLOMON: Hello, I'm Solomon Caldwell. Welcome to the Perfect Pair Competition. Wait . . . don't I know you from somewhere? What was your name? Bob?

TOM: Start with BOB and make a new word by changing only one letter. Then make another word from that word. Keep going as long as you can, but make sure my name is in there somewhere.

BOB

— — —

— — —

— — —

— — —

— — —

— — —

— — —

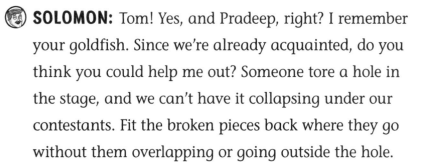 **SOLOMON:** Tom! Yes, and Pradeep, right? I remember your goldfish. Since we're already acquainted, do you think you could help me out? Someone tore a hole in the stage, and we can't have it collapsing under our contestants. Fit the broken pieces back where they go without them overlapping or going outside the hole.

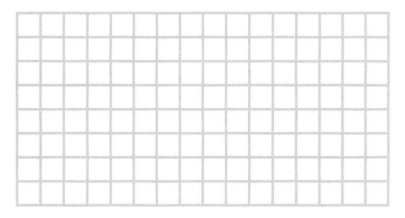

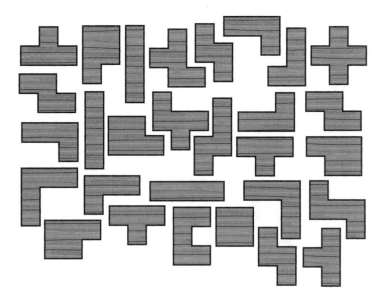

TOM: What's next?

 SOLOMON: Someone has broken the stand for our lights. See if you can build a new one out of eighteen blocks. Make sure each light has a block beneath it.

143

SOLOMON: While the staff works on the lights, I need the stage to be cleaned. They've done some of the work already, but I need as much cleaned as possible.

PRADEEP: Without taking your pencil tip off the page, draw one path that covers as much of the stage as possible. Make sure your line never crosses over itself, and the lines on the stage *have* to be part of your finished path. When you're done, Frankie can skate over everything with some suds, and we'll have it cleaned in no time.

SOLOMON: Someone has stolen the seating chart! Luckily, we have backups for everything but the first row, but that's the most problematic. We have to make sure that fishes and birds aren't beside cats, cats aren't beside dogs, and goats aren't beside turtles (they fight over the lettuce). When you've figured it out, just write everyone's name on these reservation cards, and we'll be ready to start the show!

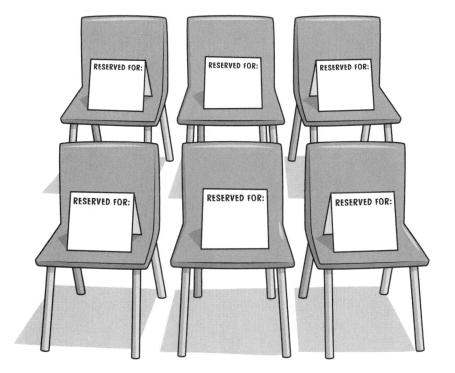

PAIRS: Tom & Frankie, Mark & Fang, Geeky Girl & Boris, Sami & Toby, Michael & His Dog, Ginger & Her Goat.

SOLOMON: After a full day of events, it's time to reveal our contestants for the pet fair's final award: the Perfect Pair! This award goes to the person and pet who are perfect for each other and have demonstrated their extraordinary connection over the course of today's fair. But first, I must reveal our *secret judges*, who have been watching our young contestants throughout the day.

TOM: No way! I didn't know they were going to have secret judges. I figured we'd have to do some kind of presentation or something.

PRADEEP: This is good. It means Mark can't make up something that wins.

GEEKY GIRL: Who do you think they voted for?

SOLOMON: They have each submitted a list of pairs they think deserve to be considered for this prize. We have added everything together, and we have our final two nominees.

PRADEEP: Who do you think it will be?

☐ Geeky Girl & Boris

☐ Tom & Frankie

☐ Ginger & Her Goat

☐ Sami & Toby

☐ Mark & Fang

☐ Michael & His Dog

SOLOMON: Our first pair is . . .

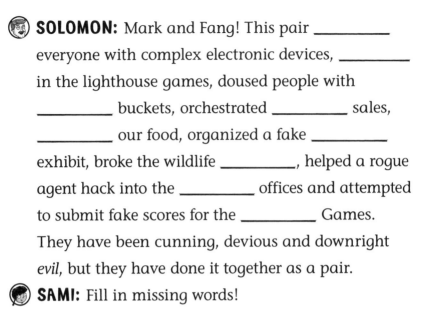 **SOLOMON:** Mark and Fang! This pair _____ everyone with complex electronic devices, _____ in the lighthouse games, doused people with _____ buckets, orchestrated _____ sales, _____ our food, organized a fake _____ exhibit, broke the wildlife _____, helped a rogue agent hack into the _____ offices and attempted to submit fake scores for the _____ Games. They have been cunning, devious and downright _evil_, but they have done it together as a pair.

 **SAMI:** Fill in missing words!

SOLOMON: Our second pair is . . .

SOLOMON: Tom and Frankie! This pair _____ everyone by rewiring their _____, won fairly in the _____, visited every _____ booth, volunteered at the _____, helped prepare _____, spread educational pamphlets about _____, expertly navigated the _____, thwarted a devious _____ in the administration building and performed admirably in the _____ Games. They have been helpful, courteous and in every way, the *good guys*, and they have done it as a pair. Not to mention, they volunteered as guides for newcomers to the fair.

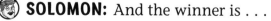 **SAMI:** Fill in missing words!

SOLOMON: And the winner is . . .

MARK: Wait! Judges, please check under your chairs. Those are copies of some files from the pet shelter . . . that I definitely did *not* steal. I think you'll find them . . . convincing. MWA-HA-HA-HA-HAAA!

FANG: MEW-MEW-MEW-MEEEW!

TOM: Can they do that?

GEEKY GIRL: Isn't that cheating?

PRADEEP: There's nothing in the rules against it.

Dear Judges for Perfect Pet Pair Contest,

I think my pet kitten, Fang, is the perfect match for me for lots of reasons.

1. She is seriously the most evil pet I've ever seen.
2. She fits perfectly in the pocket of my Evil Scientist coat.
3. She bites me less than she does anyone else.
4. She has a wicked evil meow that goes perfectly with my awesome evil laugh. Mwa-ha- ha-ha-ha-haaa.
5. We were just meant to be together, OK.

You may have heard of me if you follow Evil Science stuff. But just in case you haven't, I'll just tell you the two things about me that you really need to know. One, I'm a wickedly bad Evil Scientist (and by that I mean I'm really, really good at it. I thought I might need to explain, because as judges you are probably very old, and old people don't tend to know this stuff). Two, I am totally the perfect pet pair for Fang because she is wickedly evil too.

I got the records on Fang from the cat rescue center where she was left. (They really should lock up the windows and file cabinets at that place.) I think that these prove that she is the perfect evil kitten to be the pet of an Evil Scientist. So Fang and I should win your stupid contest and get the prize.

Sincerely (and Evilly),
Mark and Fang

P.S. If you don't pick us, whatever you do, don't pick the moron fish and my brother!
P.P.S. Or that Geeky Girl and her bird!
P.P.P.S. Or Sanj, if he steals an animal and pretends it's his!
P.P.P.P.S. Just pick me and Fang.

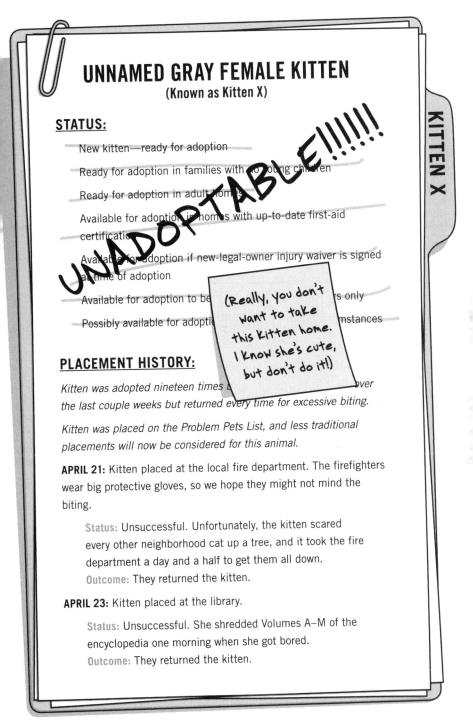

UNNAMED GRAY FEMALE KITTEN
(Known as Kitten X)

UNADOPTABLE!!!!!!

STATUS:

~~New kitten—ready for adoption~~

~~Ready for adoption in families with young children~~

~~Ready for adoption in adult homes~~

~~Available for adoption in homes with up-to-date first-aid certification~~

~~Available for adoption if new-legal-owner injury waiver is signed at time of adoption~~

(Really, you don't want to take this kitten home. I know she's cute, but don't do it!)

~~Available for adoption to be _____s only~~

~~Possibly available for adoption _____ circumstances~~

PLACEMENT HISTORY:

Kitten was adopted nineteen times _____ over the last couple weeks but returned every time for excessive biting.

Kitten was placed on the Problem Pets List, and less traditional placements will now be considered for this animal.

APRIL 21: Kitten placed at the local fire department. The firefighters wear big protective gloves, so we hope they might not mind the biting.

> Status: Unsuccessful. Unfortunately, the kitten scared every other neighborhood cat up a tree, and it took the fire department a day and a half to get them all down.
> Outcome: They returned the kitten.

APRIL 23: Kitten placed at the library.

> Status: Unsuccessful. She shredded Volumes A–M of the encyclopedia one morning when she got bored.
> Outcome: They returned the kitten.

151

APRIL 24: Kitten was placed at the local bus station.

> Status: Unsuccessful. Who knew that kitten teeth could puncture tires like that?
> Outcome: They returned the kitten.

APRIL 25: Kitten was adopted by a parachuting club.

> Status: Unsuccessful. This did not end well. Full details not supplied.
> Outcome: Kitten returned.

APRIL 26: Kitten was then placed at a l⌀

> Status: She caused a stampede o⌀
> Outcome: Kitten returned.

APRIL 27: At visiting circus.

> Status: She caused a stampede of el⌀
> Outcome: Kitten returned.

APRIL 28: At local pet store.

> Status: She caused a stampede ⌀ en know it was possible to get guin⌀
> Outcome: Kitten returned and returned and r⌀

Proof that this kitten causes as much chaos as I do (well nearly), plus she's had 27 owners, and no one has managed to keep her happy but me. So there.

APRIL 29: After much persuasion, kitten placed at the convent of the Sisters of Perpetual Patience. It is hoped that a calm and peaceful environment might have a good influence on her behavior.

> Status: Very, very unsuccessful. Unfortunately, the kitten caused the Mother Superior to break her ten-year vow of silence when the kitten hid in her wimple during Morning Prayer.
> Outcome: Kitten returned (but the convent said they would pray for us all).

Kitten returned a total of twenty-seven times. (This is a record for ANY cat home ANYWHERE!)

ANIMAL BEHAVIOR REPORT ON KITTEN X

Ability to get along with people	F–
Ability to get along with other pets	F–
Ability to respect property and surroundings	F–
follow instructions	F–
Ability to look cute	A+

This is almost exactly like the behavior report on my sixth grade report card.

COMMENTS: This kitten not only bites the hand that feeds it but then other hand that you are usi the kitten's mouth off your NEVER adopt this cat!!

(Except maybe switch the words "pets" with "kids" and switch "cute" for "cool.")

INITIAL REPORT ON KITTEN X

Left on doorstep of cat home wrapped in a black cape with this note attached.

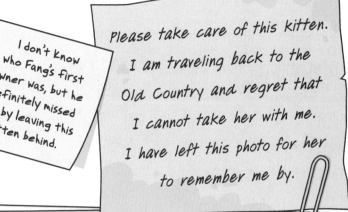

I don't know who Fang's first owner was, but he definitely missed out by leaving this kitten behind.

Please take care of this kitten. I am traveling back to the Old Country and regret that I cannot take her with me. I have left this photo for her to remember me by.

SOLOMON: This certainly changes things. Let me confer with the judges.

 **GEEKY GIRL:** Who do you think won?

SOLOMON: We have made our decision. The winner of the Perfect Pair Award is . . .

SOLOMON: A TIE! Our fantastic nominees will be sharing this lovely gold-plated trophy, which their mother has informed me will be staying in the living room. The prize money will, of course, be donated to the pet shelters of their choosing. I want to thank everyone again for coming out to this fabulous pet fair, and I wish you all good night!

TOM: Wait! We got so caught up in chasing and beating Mark, I completely forgot. You came all this way for a pet fair, and we didn't even get you a pet!

PRADEEP: What kind of pet do you want?

☐ DOG   ☐ BIRD

☐ CAT   ☐ SNAKE

☐ FISH   ☐ LIZARD

☐ RABBIT   ☐ OTHER: _____

TOM: What kind of powers do they have?

☐ Flying   ☐ Fire-breathing

☐ Invisibility   ☐ Super strength

☐ Teleporting   ☐ Zombie

☐ Stretching   ☐ Other: _____

SAMI: What is their name?

_____

PRADEEP: Where did the pet shelter find them?

_____

_____

_____

_____

GEEKY GIRL: Where did they get their powers?

_____

_____

_____

_____

MARK: Who is their arch-nemesis?

_____

_____

_____

_____

TOM: Draw your new pet!

ANSWERS

PAGE 2: WORD SEARCH

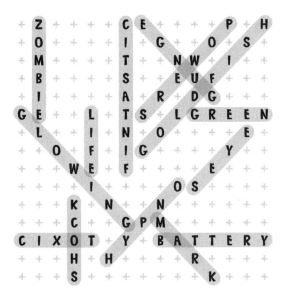

PAGE 3: HIDDEN PHRASE

SWISHYLI**Y**TTLEFISHYSWISHYLITTL**O**EFISH
YSWISHYLI**U**TTLEFISHY**H**SWISHYL**A**ITT
LEFISHYSWISHYLITTLEFISHYSW**V**ISHYLIT
TLEF**E**ISHYSWISHYLITTLEFISHYSWISHYLITT

LEF**B**SHYSWIS**E**HYLITTLEFISHYSWISHYLITTL
EFISHY**E**SWISHYL**N**ITTLEF**H**ISHYSWI**Y**SHY
LITTLEFISHYSWISHYLITTLEFISHYSWISHY**P**LI
TTLE**N**FISH**O**YSWISHYLITTLEFISHYSWISHY
LITTLEFISHYSWIS**T**HYLITI**T**LEFIS**Z**HYSWI
S**E**HYLITTLEFISHYSWISHYL**D**ITTLEFISHY

"You have been hypnotized."

PAGE 4: SPOT THE DIFFERENCE

PAGE 6: TRIVIA

1) Yellow

2) Red

3) —· —· ··——

4) Olympic Flag

5) Double Pirate Flag

PAGES 8-9: MAZE

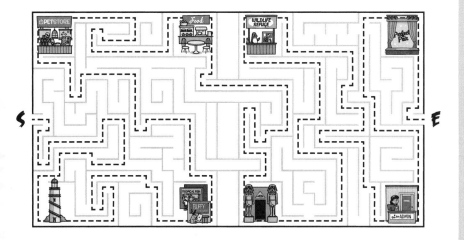

PAGE 10: ANAGRAMS

RALNPRAAOM STPE → PARANORMAL PETS

STETRNIE GUORP → INTEREST GROUP

EKEGY RILG → GEEKY GIRL

OIRBS EHT UGIDBE → BORIS THE BUDGIE

CORNRE ROTES → CORNER STORE

CMTOUERP RCEAHK → COMPUTER HACKER

CRIOAPNYCS → CONSPIRACY

PAGE 12: CRYPTOGRAPHY

"Paranormal Pets Interest Group. For pets with special, unnatural or inconvenient powers."

PAGE 13: ANAGRAMS

Although you can make many words from these letters, the answer is **computer**.

PAGE 14: WIRING

There are multiple solutions to this puzzle. The solution above is an example.

PAGE 15: PIXEL DRAWING

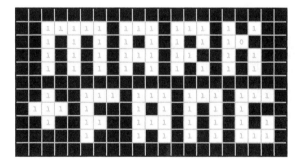

PAGE 16: CONNECT THE DOTS

PAGE 17: PIXEL DRAWING

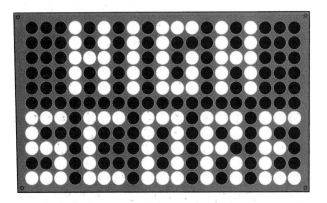

There are multiple solutions to this activity. The solution above is an example.

PAGE 19: PATHFINDING

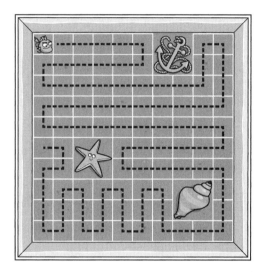

There are multiple solutions to this activity. The solution above is an example.

PAGES 20–21: REFLECTOR

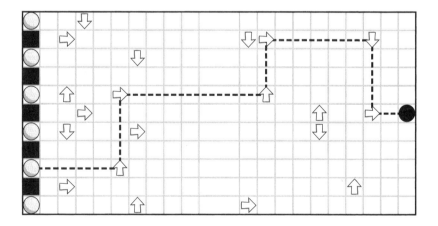

PAGE 25: BLOCK BUILDING

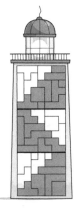

There are multiple solutions to this puzzle. The solution above is an example.

PAGE 30: CROSSWORD

ACROSS

3. Molly the Invisible <u>POODLE</u>.

4. Henry the Time-Travelling <u>HAMSTER</u>.

6. Tap-Dancing Blue-Footed <u>BOOBY</u>.

7. Camille and her Tropical <u>FISH</u>.

DOWN

1. Charlie the Painting <u>DOG</u>.

2. Tugger the Magical <u>FERRET</u>.

5. Siegfried and Roy the Roller-Skating <u>RABBITS</u>.

6. Fluffy the Psychic <u>BUNNY</u>.

PAGE 34: CRYPTOGRAPHY

"My tap-dancing teacher is missing."

PAGE 37: CONNECT THE DOTS

PAGE 47: WORD SEARCH

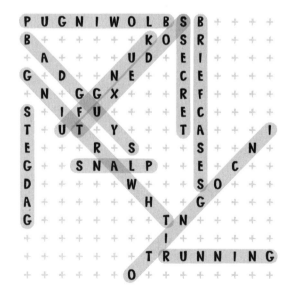

PAGES 50–51: MAZE

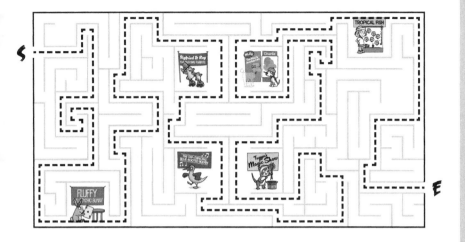

PAGE 54: ANAGRAMS

YUB TOW LSHEASE, TGE NEO ERFE → Buy Two
Leashes, Get One Free

EWN URMIAAQUS → New Aquariums

ERFE TEP SRTAET THWI CEHPSAUR → Free Pet
Treats with Purchase

EPT TEROS OGBOMTHEA → Pet Store Megabooth

WNE WEDRARS RACD → New Rewards Card

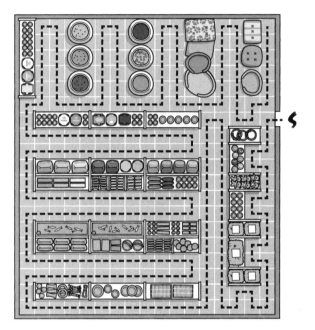

There are multiple solutions to this puzzle. The solution above is an example.

PAGE 56: LOGIC PUZZLE

PHIL: 4th person in line

REBECCA: 1st person in line

JOHN: 6th person in line

SARAH: 3rd person in line

BOBBY: 5th person in line

EMILY: 2nd person in line

PAGE 60: FIND THEM ALL

PAGE 61: WIRING

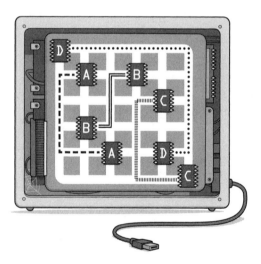

There are multiple solutions to this puzzle. The solution above is an example.

PAGE 62: LETTER BOX

“MEGABOOTH”

PAGE 63: CRYPTOGRAPHY

“Courtesy of Mark and Fang”

PAGE 64: MATCHING

1. Laser gun
2. Chemistry set
3. Suction cups
4. Laptop
5. Large mechanical claw

PAGE 65: RIDDLES

A shadow.

PAGE 67: HIDDEN PHRASE

MWAHAHAHAHAAAMW**B**AHAHAHAH
AAA**I**MWAHAHAHAHAAAMWAHAHA
GHAHAAAMWAHAH**B**AHAHAAAMWA**R**
HAHAHAHAA**O**AMWAHAHAHAHAAA
MWAH**T**AHAHAHAAAM**H**WAHAHAH**E**A

HAAAMWAHAHAH**R**AHAAAMWAHAHA
SHAHAAAM**A**WAHAHAHAHAAAMW**R**A
HAHAHAHAAA**E**MWAHAHAHAHAA**S**A
MWAHAHAHA**T**HAAAMW**U**AHAHAHA
HA**P**AAMWAHAHAHAHAAAMWAH**I**A
HAHAHAAAMWAHAHAHAHAA**D**AMW
AHAHAHAHAAAMWAHAHAHAHAAA

"Big brothers are stupid."

PAGE 68: SPOT THE DIFFERENCE

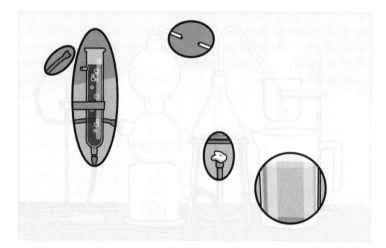

PAGES 70–71: PUT THINGS IN ORDER

2, 3, 4, 1, 8, 6, 5, 9, 10, 7, 11

PAGE 73: CROSSWORD

1. Electricity
2. Gunge
3. Evil
4. Laser
5. Scientist

6. Kidnap
7 ACROSS. Lair
7 DOWN. Lab coat
8. Chemistry
9. Plan

PAGE 76: WORD SEARCH

PAGE 77: FRANKIE'S FOOD

PAGE 78: PIXEL DRAWING

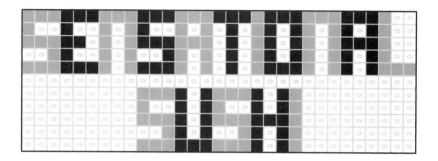

"SENSATIONAL SUSHI"

PAGE 79: THREE CUTS

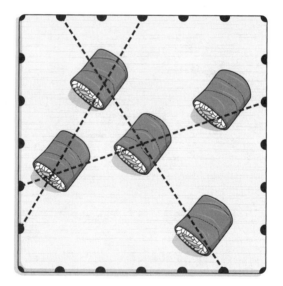

There are multiple solutions to this puzzle. The solution above is an example.

PAGE 85: WIRING

There are multiple solutions to this puzzle. The solution above is an example.

PAGE 87: BUFFET TRAYS

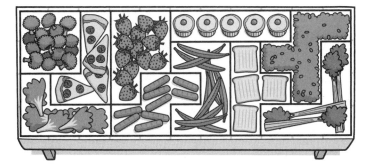

PAGE 88: MAZE

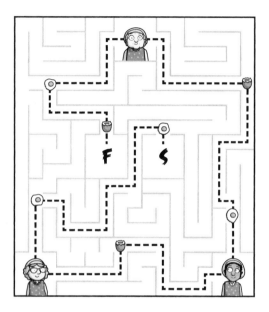

PAGE 91: CONNECT THE DOTS

PAGE 92: ANAGRAMS

MOST COMMON ANSWER: Bastet

PAGE 93: RIDDLES

1. A person
2. Nothing
3. Corn (Fish also works, just not around Frankie!)
4. Empty

PAGE 96: TWO CUTS

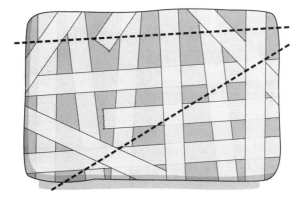

There are multiple solutions to this puzzle. The solution above is an example.

PAGE 98: CRYPTOGRAPHY

"Bow down before the mighty Fang!"

PAGE 99: ANAGRAM

"All of this Egyptian stuff is fake! Mark was the one who sent it!"

PAGE 100: RIPPED PAPER

PAGE 101: TRIVIA

1. The Emerald-Eyed Protector
2. 4
3. Take care of them in the afterlife.
4. Tastes awful

PAGES 102–103: MAZE

PAGES 104–105: CROSSWORD

ACROSS
1. clover
2. carefully
5. exposed
7. tough
8. attack
10. strike
12. return
14. kelp

DOWN
1. colder
3. alone
4. mistakes
6. poison
9. alert
11. freak
13. tool

PAGE 106: SPOT THE DIFFERENCE

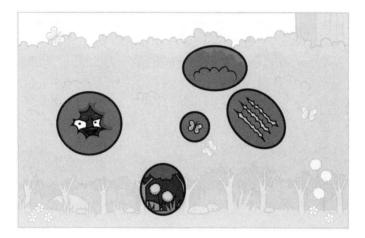

PAGE 108: MATCHING

In critters will creep if you store food where you sleep.

Never try to outrun a bear. He's faster than you, so don't you dare.

Critters with cubs will always protect them, so don't pick one up and don't try to pet 'em.

Never touch anything in a bird's nest. Leave it alone. Give it a rest.

If you see a night animal during the day, it could be sick with rabies, so keep far away!

Fire salamanders are full of venom. Best stay far away and don't try to inspect them.

Rattlesnakes rattle when you get too close.
What does its bite do? Well, trust me. It's gross.

The platypus looks so cuddly and sweet, but
the males have venomous spikes in their feet.

PAGES 110–111: BROKEN MAZE

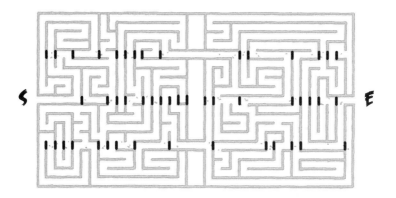

PAGE 112: BLOCK BUILDING

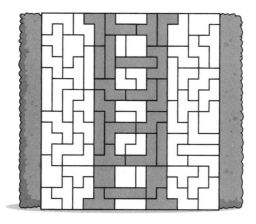

There are multiple solutions to this puzzle. The solution above is an example.

PAGE 115: WIRING

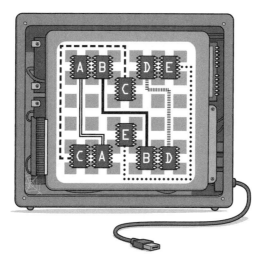

There are multiple solutions to this puzzle. The solution above is an example.

PAGE 121: MAZE

PAGE 124: HIDDEN PHRASE

BIGBROTHER**R**SEVILDEEDSTOLITTLE
ANNOYINGMORONS**B**BIGBROTHER
SEVILDEEDSTOLITTLEANNOYING**M**M
ORONSB**B**IGBROTHERSEVILDEEDST
OLITTLEANNOYINGMORONSBIGB
ROTHERSEVIL**L**DEEDSTOL**L**ITTLEANN
OYINGMORONS**S**BIGBROTHERSEVIL
DEED**D**STOLITTLE**E**ANNOYINGMORONS
BIGBROTHERS**E**EVILDEEDSTOLITTLEA
NNO**U**YINGMORONSBIGBROTHERSEVI
LDEEDSTOLITTLEA**A**NNOYINGMORONS

Letters: **R B M B L L S D E E U A**

PAGE 125: ANAGRAM

There are *hundreds* of possible words you can
make from these letters, but Sanj's password is
"B.B.E.D.L.A.M. RULES."

PAGES 126–127: PUT IN ORDER

7, 9, 2, 5, 10, 3, 6, 4, 8, 1, 11

PAGE 128: WORD SEARCH

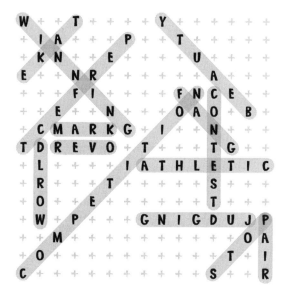

PAGES 134–135: REFLECTOR

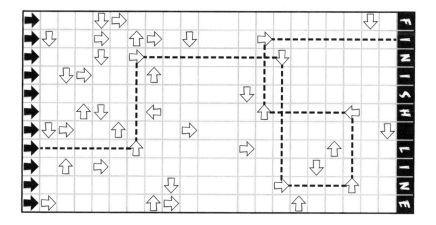

PAGE 140: TRIVIA

1. Principles of Knighthood
2. gallant and well-mannered
3. very unchivalrous
4. report it to the judges
5. A, B and C

PAGE 142: STAGE FLOOR

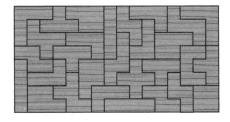

There are multiple solutions to this puzzle. The solution above is an example.

PAGE 143: BLOCK BUILDING

There are multiple solutions to this puzzle. The solution above is an example.

PAGE 144: PATHFINDING

There are multiple solutions to this puzzle. The solution above is an example.

PAGE 145: LOGIC PUZZLE

Mark & Fang   Ginger & Her Goat   Tom & Frankie

Geeky Girl & Boris   Sami & Toby   Michael & His Dog

PAGE 148: FILL IN THE BLANKS

scrambled	fake	maze
cheated	poisoned	administration
water	Egyptian	Olym-Pets

PAGE 149: FILL IN THE BLANKS

unscrambled	pet store	IT guy
computers	food	Olym-Pets
lighthouse games	Ancient Egypt	
indie	wildlife maze